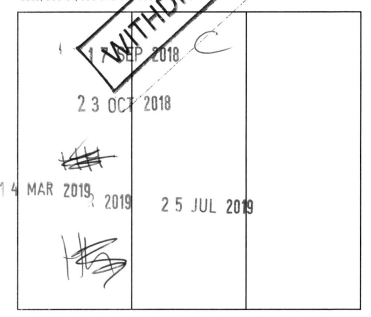

THE PADDINGTON MYSTERY

'THE DETECTIVE STORY CLUB is a clearing house for the best detective and mystery stories chosen for you by a select committee of experts. Only the most ingenious crime stories will be published under the THE DETECTIVE STORY CLUB imprint. A special distinguishing stamp appears on the wrapper and title page of every THE DETECTIVE STORY CLUB book—the Man with the Gun. Always look for the Man with the Gun when buying a Crime book.'

Wm. Collins Sons & Co. Ltd., 1929

Now the Man with the Gun is back in this series of COLLINS CRIME CLUB reprints, and with him the chance to experience the classic books that influenced the Golden Age of crime fiction.

THE DETECTIVE STORY CLUB

FURTHER TITLES IN PREPARATION

THE PADDINGTON MYSTERY

A STORY OF CRIME

BY

JOHN RHODE

PLUS
'THE PURPLE LINE'

WITH AN INTRODUCTION BY
TONY MEDAWAR

COLLINS
CRIME
CLUB

COLLINS CRIME CLUB

An imprint of HarperCollins*Publishers*
1 London Bridge Street
London SE1 9GF
www.harpercollins.co.uk

This Detective Story Club edition 2018

1

First published in Great Britain by Geoffrey Bles 1925
'The Purple Line' first published in the *Evening Standard* 1950

Copyright © Estate of John Rhode 1925, 1950
Introduction © Tony Medawar 2018

A catalogue record for this book is available from the British Library

ISBN 978-0-00-826884-8

Typeset in Bulmer MT Std by
Palimpsest Book Production Ltd, Falkirk, Stirlingshire

Printed and bound in Great Britain by CPI Group (UK) Ltd,
Croydon CR0 4YY

INTRODUCTION

THE writer best known as 'John Rhode' was born Cecil John Charles Street on 3 May 1884 in the British territory of Gibraltar. His mother was descended from a wealthy Yorkshire family and his father was a distinguished Commander in the British Army who—at the time of his son's birth—was serving in Gibraltar as Colonel-in-Chief of the Second Battalion of Scottish Rifles.

Shortly after his birth John Street's parents returned to England where, not long after John's fifth birthday, his father died unexpectedly. John and his widowed mother went to live with her father, and in 1895 John was sent to Wellington College in Berkshire. John did well in his academic studies and, perhaps unsurprisingly given the approach he took to detective stories, he excelled in the sciences. At the age of 16, John left school to attend the Royal Military Academy at Woolwich and, on the outbreak of the Great War, as it was then called, he enlisted, rising to the rank of Major by March 1918. While he was wounded three times, John Street's main contribution to the war effort concerned the promulgation of allied propaganda, for which he was awarded the Order of the British Empire in the New Year Honours List for 1918 and also the prestigious Military Cross. As the war came to an end John Street moved to a new propaganda role in Dublin Castle in Ireland, where he would be responsible for countering the campaigning of the Irish nationalists during the so-called war of Irish independence. But the winds of change were blowing across Ireland and the resolution—or rather the *partial* resolution—of the 'Irish Question' would soon come in the form of a treaty and the partition of the island of Ireland. As history was made, Street was its chronicler, at least from the British perspective.

During the 1920s, other than making headlines for falling down a lift shaft, John Street spent most of his time at a typewriter, producing a fictionalised memoir of the war and political studies of France, Germany, Hungary and Czechoslovakia, as well as two biographies. He also wrote a few short stories and articles on an eclectic range of subjects including piracy, camouflage and concealment, Slovakian railways, the value of physical exercise, peasant art, telephony, and the challenges of post-war reconstruction. He even found time to enter crossword competitions and, reflecting his keen interest in what is now known as 'true crime', he published the first full-length study of the trial of Constance Kent, who was convicted for one of the most gruesome murders of the nineteenth century at Road House in Kent. John also found time to write three thrillers and a wartime romance. However, while his early books found some success, the Golden Age of detective stories had arrived, and he decided to try *his* hand at the genre.

The first challenge was to create a great detective, someone to rival the likes of Roger Sheringham and Hercule Poirot, with whose creators John Street would soon be on first name terms. Street's great detective was the almost supernaturally intelligent Lancelot Priestley, a former academic, who in the words of the critic Howard Haycraft was 'fairly well along in years, without a sense of humour and inclined to dryness'. Dr Priestley's first case, published in October 1925, would be *The Paddington Mystery*. Doctor—or rather Professor—Priestley was an immediate success, and Street was quick to respond, producing another six novels in short order. As well as Priestley, Street's 'John Rhode' novels often feature one or both of two Scotland Yard detectives, Inspector Hanslet and Inspector Jimmy Waghorn who would in later years appear without Priestley in several radio plays and a short stage play.

By 1930, John Street was no longer just a highly decorated former Army Major with a distinguished career in military intelligence—he had now written a total of 25 books under various pseudonyms. He was 45 years old, and he was just getting started. As 'John Rhode' he would produce a total of 76 novels, all but five of which feature Dr Priestley and one of which was based on the notorious Wallace case. But, while writing as 'John Rhode', Street also became 'Miles Burton', under which pseudonym he wrote 63 novels featuring Desmond Merrion, a retired naval officer who may well have been named after Merrion Street in Dublin. There also exists an unfinished and untitled final novel, inspired it would appear by the famous Green Bicycle Case. The 'Rhode' and 'Burton' detective mysteries are similar, but whereas Priestley is generally dry and unemotional, Merrion is more of a gentleman sleuth in the manner of Philip Trent or Lord Peter Wimsey. Both Merrion and Priestley are engaged from time to time by Scotland Yard acquaintances, all of whom are portrayed respectfully rather than as the servile and unimaginative policemen created by some of Street's contemporaries.

But two pseudonyms weren't enough and, astonishingly, 'Rhode' also became 'Cecil Waye', a fact that was only discovered long after his death. For the four 'Cecil Waye' books, Street created two new series characters—the brother and sister team of Christopher and Vivienne Perrin, two investigators rather in the mould of Agatha Christie's 'Young Adventurers', Tommy and Tuppence Beresford. The Perrins would appear in four novels, which are now among the rarest of John Street's books. Curiously, the first 'Cecil Waye' title—*Murder at Monk's Barn*— is a detective story very much in the style that he would use for most of his 'John Rhode' and 'Miles Burton' books. However, the other three are metropolitan thrillers, with less than convincing plots, especially the best-known, *The Prime Minister's Pencil.*

As well as writing detective stories, John Street was also a member of the Detection Club, the illustrious dining club whose purpose, in Street's words, was for detective story writers 'to dine together at stated intervals for the purpose of discussing matters concerned with their craft'. As one of the founding members, Street's most important contribution was the creation of Eric the Skull, which—showing that he had not lost his youthful technical skills—he wired up with lights so that the eye sockets glowed red during the initiation ceremony for new members. Eric the Skull still participates in the rituals by which new members are admitted to the Detection Club. Street also edited *Detection Medley*, the first and arguably best anthology of stories by members of the Club, and he contributed to the Club's first two round-robin detective novels, *The Floating Admiral* and *Ask a Policeman*, as well as the excellent true crime anthology *The Anatomy of Murder* and one of their series of detective radio plays. Street was also happy to help other Detection Club members with scientific and technical aspects of their own work, including those giants of the genre Dorothy L. Sayers and John Dickson Carr; in fact Carr later made Street the inspiration for his character Colonel March, head of *The Department of Queer Complaints*.

In an authoritative and essential study of some of the lesser luminaries of the Golden Age, the American writer Curtis Evans described John Street as 'the master of murder means' and praised his 'fiendish ingenuity [in] the creative application of science and engineering'. For Street is *genuinely* ingenious, devising seemingly impossible crimes in locked houses, locked bathrooms and locked railway compartments, and even—in *Drop to his Death* (co-authored with Carr)—a locked elevator. Who else but Street could come up with the idea of using a hedgehog as a murder weapon? A marrow? A hot water bottle? Even bed-sheets and pyjamas are lethal in his hands.

Street's books are also noteworthy for their humour and social observations, and he doesn't shy from defying some of the expectations of the genre: in one novel Dr Priestley allows a murderer to go free, and in another the guilty party is identified and put on trial . . . but acquitted.

John Street died on 8 December 1964. Half a century later, while he is not as highly regarded by critics as, say, Christie, Carr or Sayers, he remains one of the most popular writers of the Golden Age, producing more than 140 of what one fan neatly described as 'pure and clever detective stories'. Not a bad epitaph.

TONY MEDAWAR
November 2017

CHAPTER I

'Steady, sir!' exclaimed the taxi-driver sharply.

Harold Merefield made a wild clutch at the open door of the vehicle and managed to save himself from falling into the roadway.

'It—it's all right,' he stammered. 'Beastly shlippery tonight, must be a frost. Wosher fare?'

The taxi-driver lit a match and gazed speculatively at his clock. The young toff was too far gone to have any inkling of time or distance.

'Eight and ninepence,' he declared, with the air of a man who states an ascertained and incontrovertible fact.

Harold Merefield fumbled in his pocket and produced a ten-shilling note. 'Here you are,' he said magnificently. 'I don't want any change.'

He suddenly let go of the door handle, as though it had become too hot for him to hold, and started off rapidly down the Harrow Road. The taxi-driver watched his course with an appraising eye.

'That's a rum set-out,' he muttered. 'Bloke picks me up in Piccadilly at 'alf past two in the morning, and tells me to drive 'im to Paddington Register Office. Drunk as a lord, too. An' when I takes 'im there, blowed if 'e don't make tracks straight for the perlice station, like as though he wants to give 'imself up for drunk and disorderly. No, he don't, though, he's got 'is wits about 'im more than I gave 'im credit for. Well, it's no concern o' mine. Time I 'opped it.'

He put his lever into gear, swung his wheel round, and disappeared in the direction of the Edgware Road.

The object of his solicitude, although he had certainly set out towards the police station, had turned off to the left past

1

the gate of the casual ward of the workhouse, planting his feet with the severe determination of one who dares his conscience to declare that he is drunk. It was obvious that he had often trodden this way before; an onlooker, had there been such, might have gained the impression that his legs, accustomed to this route, needed no guidance from a bemused brain. They steered an uncertain course down the middle of the road taking corners warily, like a ship swinging round a buoy, and turned at last into a narrow cul-de-sac adorned with a battered sign upon which, by daylight, might have been deciphered 'Riverside Gardens.'

But, as it happened, there were no onlookers, as was perhaps natural at three a.m. of a winter's night. The evening had been foggy; one of those late November evenings when a general gloom settles down upon London, producing not the merry blind-man's-buff of a true pea-souper, but an irritating, choking opacity through which the gas-lamps show as vague blurs of light, beneath which the shadowy traffic roars and jolts. A thoroughly unpleasant evening, making the luxury of warmly-carpeted rooms, illuminated discreetly by shaded electric lamps, seem all the more desirable by contrast with the chill discomfort of the cheerless streets.

So Harold Merefield had felt as he had entered the portals of the Naxos Club, that retiring establishment which veiled its seductions behind the dingy brick front of an upper part in a modest Soho street. Upon leaving it his reflections were no longer meteorological, but it was somehow borne in upon him that the fog had lifted, to be replaced by a fine and exceedingly chilly drizzle. Having found a taxi, and persuaded the fellow that he really did want to be driven to the Paddington Register Office—a matter of some difficulty, since the man had expressed disgusted scorn at such a destination—"'Ere, come off it. 'Tain't open at this time o' night, and besides, you ain't got no girl with you'—he had flung himself down into the corner, the easier to meditate upon his grievance. Oh, yes, it had been a jolly night enough, he was ready to admit that, jolly enough for the other fellows, that is. His own evening had been spoilt, for what was the fun of drinking by oneself, or with such of the girls who chose to offer themselves as temporary solaces to his loneliness? Vere, who had never before failed him, had unaccountably absented herself, without a word of warning, without even ringing him up to make her excuses. Of course, he might have gone to her rooms and fetched her, but why the devil should he, on a night like that? He wasn't going to run after any girl, she could come or not as she chose. Next time he wouldn't turn up himself, and we'd see how she liked that.

The stopping of the taxi had interrupted the train of his thought. His stumbling exit provided him with a new sense of grievance, as he became conscious that he had barked his shins. He felt himself a deeply ill-used man as he turned into Riverside Gardens and splashed unsteadily through the puddles which had collected on its disreputable paving. On either side of the short road, a backwater, hidden away in this remoter part of Paddington, the unkempt front gardens of a row of tumble-down two-storied houses stood, dark and smelling of the rubbish they harboured. He passed them all, and turned in through the gateway in the low wall of the last garden on the right-hand side. He had reached home safely.

Number 16, Riverside Gardens was, perhaps, the least decayed of the row that bore this surprising name. From the narrow pavement of the cul-de-sac an asphalt path some ten yards long led through what had once been a garden, but was now merely a plot of waste land covered with rubbish, to a doorway screened by a ramshackle porch. You mounted a couple of steps, and from the top of these the mystery of the name was revealed. A low wall bounded the end of the cul-de-sac and the side of the garden; on the other side of this, dank, ill-odorous and forbidding, lay the stagnant waters of the Grand Junction Canal, an inky liquid besprinkled with nameless flotsam. It only needed sufficient imagination to see in this melancholy ditch a river, and in the desolate patches of earth before the houses a wealth of vegetation and the unexpected nomenclature became obvious.

Your enquiring mind thus set at rest, you explored the doorway in front of you. You had a choice of two panels on which to rap—there was no sign of a bell, merely the narrow orifice of a Yale lock on either door. One of these doors led into what was known by courtesy as 'The Shop'; so much you could guess by peering through the filthy panes of the window on your left. Above this door you might have deciphered the name 'G. Boost.' From your necessarily limited survey through the window you would probably gather that Mr Boost's shop was devoted to the accumulation of all the rubbish that the march of progress has banished from the Victorian middle-class home.

It was into the lock of the other door that Harold Merefield, not without some difficulty, occasioned by the reluctance of his hand to find the more distinct of the images conveyed to his brain by his eyes, inserted his key. The door swung open, revealing a narrow flight of stairs, rather surprisingly covered with a worn but excellent carpet. These heavily surmounted, the tenant of this curious dwelling reached a small landing, off which two doors led. He opened that towards the front of the house, stumbled in, knocked clumsily against various pieces of furniture, and at length, after much vain groping, accompanied by muttered curses, found a box of matches and struck a light. This done, he flung his coat in a heap upon the floor, and sank into a remarkably comfortable and well-cushioned chair.

The spectacle of a young man in impeccable evening dress sitting in a luxuriously-furnished room in the heart of a particularly ill-favoured slum might reasonably have been considered a remarkable portent. But then, Harold Merefield—his name, by the way, was pronounced Merryfield, a circumstance which had led to his being known as 'Merry Devil' to certain of his boon companions at the Naxos Club—was, in every respect, a remarkable young man. It had always been understood that he was to succeed his father, an elderly widower and a respected family solicitor, in his provincial practice. However, on the outbreak of war he had secured a commission, and had served until the Armistice without distinction but with satisfaction to himself and his superior officers.

Meanwhile his father had died, leaving far less than his only child had confidently expected. And on demobilisation Harold had found himself possessed of a small income, of which he could not touch the capital, an instinctive dislike of the prospect of hard work, and a promising taste for dissipation. His problem was so to reconcile these three factors as to gain the greatest pleasure from existence. He solved it in his own fashion. There were reasons which drew him towards London, and particularly towards Paddington. By a curious chance he saw the notice 'Rooms to Let' painted in sprawling letters on a board propped up in Mr Boost's front garden. The idea tickled him; he could live here in such seclusion as he pleased, spending the minimum on rent and thereby reserving the maximum for pleasure. To this unpromising retreat he moved so much of his father's furniture as the place would hold, the remainder he sold. His orbit in future was bounded by the Naxos Club on the one hand and Riverside Gardens on the other.

But sometimes, deviating slightly from this appointed path, as a comet surprises astronomers by its aberrations, he touched other planes of existence. Revelling in the content of idleness as he did, he yet felt at long intervals that irresistible itch which impels the hand towards pen and paper. The eventual result was a novel, which, with engaging candour, he himself described as tripe. Tripe indeed it was, but tripe which by the method of its preparation had acquired a pronounced gamy flavour. It dealt with the lives and loves of the peculiar stratum of society which frequented the Naxos Club. To cut a long story short, *Aspasia's Adventures* was accepted by a firm of publishers who, as the result of persistent effort, had acquired an honourable reputation for the production of this type of fiction. With certain necessary emendation, the substitution of innuendo for bald description, it was published, and brought its author a small sum in royalties, a few indignant references in the more hypocritical section of the Press, and an intimation from the publishers that they would be prepared to consider further works of a similar nature. But it brought more than this. It brought the means of quieting the last scruples of an almost anæsthetised conscience. Harold Merefield's method of life was crowned by the justification of a Career.

But it was not of his career that Harold was thinking as he lay in his comfortable chair. In fact, he found it difficult to think consecutively about anything at all. He knew that he was tired and sleepy, but the act of closing his eyes produced an unpleasant and nauseating sensation, in some way connected with rapidly-revolving wheels of fire. It wasn't so bad if he kept them open. Certainly the flame of the candle refused to be focussed, and advanced and receded in the most irritating fashion. A wave of self-pity flowed over him. He was a wretched, lonely creature. Vere had forsaken him, Vere, the girl he had given such a good time to all these months. Vere's form kept getting between him and the candle, tantalising, mocking him. Somewhere, in the dark corners of the room, another female form hovered, a reproach, a menace to his peace of mind. He laughed scornfully. Oh yes, it was all very well for April and her father to upbraid him as a rotter, to fling the authorship of *Aspasia* in his teeth. Why couldn't they say straight out that Evan Denbigh was a more desirable match for April? Damned young prig! He hadn't the guts of a louse.

For a moment his fluttering thoughts lit upon the person of Evan Denbigh. His sweeping condemnation was followed by a wave of generosity. Good fellow, Denbigh, at heart, but not at all his sort. Hardworking, clever fellow, and all that. Of course, April would prefer him to a miserable lonely devil like himself. Let her marry him; he would take his revenge by showing them what he could do. He could write a best-seller if he put his mind to it. Yes, by Jove, he'd start now.

He leapt from his chair, stood for a moment as though balancing himself on a narrow ledge, then sank back once more, dispirited. What was the use? Who cared what he did? April was beyond his reach, Vere had chucked him, the fire in the untidy grate was out long ago. There was nothing for it but to go to bed.

Very deliberately, as though embarking upon an undertaking which required skill and concentration for its successful accomplishment, he climbed out of his chair, grasped the candlestick in an unsteady hand, and staggered towards the door which led into the bedroom at the back of the house. He negotiated the narrow doorway, laid the candle down on the dressing-table, and began to fumble at his collar and tie. All at once the extreme desirability of seeking a prone position impressed itself upon him. Curse these clothes! They seemed to hang upon him as an incubus, resisting every attempt of his groping fingers to divest himself of them. He flung his coat and waistcoat upon a chair, and turned with a sigh of relief towards the bed. He must lie down for a bit, his head was beginning to ache, he could finish undressing when he felt better.

The candle threw a flickering light across the room. He could see a dark mass upon the bed, doubtless the suit he had thrown upon it when he was dressing that evening. He put out his hand to drag them off, and even as he did so stopped suddenly, as though a cold hand had gripped him. That dark mass was not his clothes at all. It was a man lying on his bed.

The first shock over and certainty established, he chuckled foolishly. A man! If it had been a woman, now! Vere, perhaps, come all this way to beg his forgiveness. Of course, it couldn't be. How could she have got in? He had given her a latchkey once, but the first thing she had done had been to lose it. How on earth had this fellow got in, then?

Harold returned to the dressing-table to fetch the candle.

This sort of thing was insufferable. Holding the candle over the bed he began to apostrophise his visitor.

'Look here, my friend, I don't so much mind finding you in my rooms like this, but I do draw the line at your turning me out of my own bed. Sleep here if you must, but sleep on the sofa next door and let me have the bed like a good fellow. I've had rather a hectic night of it.'

The form on the bed made no sign of having heard him. Harold put his hand on its shoulder and withdrew it suddenly. The clothes he had touched were oozing water. With a thrill of horror Harold bent over still further and put the candle close to the man's face. His eyes were open, glassy, staring at nothing. Shocked into horrified sobriety, Harold thrust his hand beneath the man's soaked clothing, seeking the skin above the heart. It was cold and clammy, not the slightest pulsation could he feel stirring the inert body.

For an instant he paused, fighting the sensation of physical sickness that surged through him. Then, as he was, stopping only to fling round him his discarded overcoat, he rushed from the house and dashed frantically to the police station.

CHAPTER II

IT was not until a week afterwards that Harold found leisure or courage to call upon Professor Lancelot Priestley. Leisure, because his time had been fully occupied, and that most unpleasantly, in attending the inquest and being interviewed by pertinacious officers who displayed an indecent curiosity as to his habits and acquaintances. Courage—well, Professor Priestley happened to be April's father, and they had last parted as a result of a most regrettable incident.

Professor Priestley had been a schoolfellow of his father, and the two had kept up a certain intimacy through early life. But while Merefield the elder had settled down comfortably to country solicitorship, Priestley, cursed with a restless brain and an almost immoral passion for the highest branches of mathematics, occupied himself in skirmishing round the portals of the Universities, occasionally flinging a bomb in the shape of a highly controversial thesis in some ultra-scientific journal. How long this single-handed warfare against established doctrine might have lasted there is no telling. But with characteristic unexpectedness Priestley solved his personal binomial problem by marrying a lady of some means, who, having presented him with April, conveniently died when the child was fourteen, perhaps of a surfeit of logarithms.

Upon his marriage, Priestley had settled down, to use the term in a comparative sense. That is to say, he exchanged his former guerilla warfare for a regular siege. No longer were his weapons the bayonet and the bomb; he now employed the heavy artillery of lectures and weighty articles, with which he bombarded the supporters of all accepted theory. He claimed to be the precursor of Einstein, the first to breach the citadel of Newton. And as none of his acquaintances knew anything about these matters, he was not subjected to the annoyance of contradiction in his own house.

The two friends, Merefield and Priestley, continued to see one another at frequent intervals. Priestley would take his little daughter down to stay in the country, Merefield would bring his boy up for a week in town, when April and Harold, much of an age, would be sent to the Zoo and Madame Tussaud's and Earl's Court Exhibition, under the careful tutelage of April's governess. Their parents, presumably, alternated the conversation between the calculus of variations and the rights of heirs and assigns over messuages and tenements.

It was perhaps unavoidable that one of those curious understandings, whose secrets adults fondly imagine are securely hidden from their offspring, should have been arrived at between the two. And in this case the understanding was less vague than usual. Anything indeterminate was a source of horror to the mathematician; anything loosely worded a reproach to the solicitor. It is not to be supposed that an agreement was actually drawn up, sealed, signed and delivered. But both these fond parents had firmly made up their minds that Harold was to marry April.

Their children, more accommodating than children are apt to be, fell in willingly enough with this plan. It was, of course, only conveyed to them in hints, increasing in clarity as they approached years of discretion. The whole business was taken for granted; it was a postulate to which there could be no possible alternative. Then came the war, the death of Merefield the elder, and Harold's strange aberration from his appointed path.

There is no need to trace the widening of the breach, the outspoken condemnations of Professor Priestley, the subtler scorn of April. The crisis came one afternoon, when Harold had called at the house in Westbourne Terrace after lunching particularly well. *Aspasia's Adventures* had been published a few days previously, and the occasion had called for a bottle by way of celebration. The first thing that met Harold's eye on the table of the Professor's study, into which he had been shown, was a copy of this sensational volume—it should be remarked that the publishers had seen fit to embellish it with a jacket upon which the heroine was displayed in male company in a lack of costume definitely startling. Harold's interview with April's father ended with the statement by the latter that he could not possibly contemplate the marriage of his daughter to a man whose dissipated manners had culminated in the production of such pornographic twaddle as this, to which Harold, emboldened by champagne, had retorted that April appeared to be adequately consoled by the company of that young cub Evan Denbigh, and that he proposed to go his own way as he pleased, anyhow. This short and heated interview had taken place some six months previously, and had been the last occasion on which he had passed the portals of the house in Westbourne Terrace.

But it was now a very chastened Harold who pressed the bell-push, with that nervous touch which betrays a secret hope that the bell has not rung, and that a few more minutes of respite must therefore elapse before the ordeal. But, light as had been his touch, the bell had tinkled far away in the lower regions, and Mary, the old parlourmaid, to whom much was forgiven, appeared with startling suddenness.

She, at least, was still on Harold's side, retaining, perhaps, fond memories of secret orgies of candied peel in her pantry when the children were placed temporarily in her charge in the absence of the governess.

'Gracious me, Master Harold, you are a stranger!' she exclaimed. Then, with swift recollection of the respect due to one whose name had appeared so prominently in the papers during the last few days, she continued: 'The Master's in his study, sir, if you'll kindly come this way—'

Well, he was in for it now. The door opened and he was ushered in. The Professor, working at his desk in the window, started up at the sound of his name.

'Come in, Harold, my boy,' he exclaimed, holding out his hand. 'Sit down and make yourself comfortable. I'm very glad of the opportunity of telling you how sorry we were to read of this—er—distressing occurrence.'

'Thank you, sir,' Harold replied gratefully. 'I felt I had to come round and talk to you about it.'

He sat down in one of the leather chairs before the fire, and the Professor took the other.

'I was waiting for you to come,' said the latter quietly. 'I would have come to you, but it seemed better you should come of your own accord. I think I can guess the shock it must have been to you.'

Harold paused a minute. 'I've been through a pretty rotten time in the last few days,' he replied. 'I suppose you've seen all about it in the papers?'

The Professor nodded, and Harold continued despondently.

'It's made me pretty sick with myself and the way I've been living. Although I went straight to the police, they seemed to think I was in some way responsible for the man's death. I had to answer a devil of a lot of questions as to my movements that evening. They found the taxi-driver who had driven me home; fortunately the man remembered me. But that didn't satisfy them. They wanted to know where I had been spending my time before he picked me up. I wouldn't tell them for a long time, until they pointed out that if they put me on my trial it was bound to come out.'

'Why wouldn't you tell them?' enquired the Professor.

'Well—oh, I may as well make a clean breast of it, sir,' replied Harold impulsively. 'I'd been spending the evening at a place I particularly didn't want to draw their attention to. It's called the Naxos Club—drink after hours, and all that kind of thing, you know.'

The Professor furrowed his brow in thought. 'Naxos, Naxos?' he repeated. 'Ah yes, I remember a young woman of the name of Ariadne, had an—ah—adventure with Bacchus at an island of that name some years ago. A most suitable designation for your club, no doubt. So you had to divulge the secrets of this place to the police, had you?'

'I only told them I'd been there,' replied Harold. 'Inspector Hanslet, who had charge of my case, said that if the taxi-driver was correct as to my condition when he drove me home the place would bear looking into. Next day he told me that my alibi was established, but that the members of the Naxos Club would have to seek another rendezvous in future. I'm afraid he must have had it raided.'

'I'm afraid he must,' commented the Professor drily. 'A fact which will scarcely add to your popularity with your former associates. Take my advice and drop them, my boy. It isn't too late to run straight, you know. You've had a nasty shock, and you may as well profit by it.'

'I wish to God I could!' exclaimed Harold. 'I'm sick of the whole thing, sick of the rotten way I've behaved, thoroughly well ashamed of myself. I'd like to go straight, to find a decent job somewhere, but what the devil am I to do? This man's death is still a mystery, they haven't even found out who he was. The coroner made some pretty rotten remarks at the inquest, the police and everybody else seem to think that even if I didn't kill him, I must know something about the business. No, I'm under suspicion—I know jolly well I'm being watched still. And you can't expect anyone to take kindly to a fellow whose name has been unpleasantly notorious in the papers for a week. No, sir it's no good. I shall have to clear out of the country, and that's what I came to ask you about.'

The Professor paused a minute before replying. 'I'm not surprised you look at it like that,' he said at last. 'The trouble you have have been through has not unnaturally got on your nerves. But, as a matter of fact, it is not so bad as you make out. I, for one, am completely convinced of your innocence, not because I have known you all your life, but from the logical facts of the case. Scientific reasoning is on your side, my boy.'

He paused again, and Harold muttered his thanks for this frank testimonial. Then he continued, slowly and with some deliberation, as though he were expounding a thesis.

'I agree that there are many who might be disposed to think you not altogether guiltless. The discovery of a dead man on one's bed would certainly incline loose thinkers to a suspicion that there must be some connection between oneself and the deceased. Unfortunately, this kind of thinking is so impervious to argument that the only way to refute it is by the demonstration of the true facts of the case. In this particular instance, this is the function of the police, but I very much doubt that they will proceed much further in the matter. They are solely concerned with the detection of crime. They may well argue that no crime was committed, since the result of the inquest was a verdict of "Death from natural causes". In other words, my boy, if you want to clear yourself in the eyes of the world, you will have to unravel the mystery yourself.'

'That's very much the conclusion I came to myself,' replied Harold disconsolately. 'But I haven't the least idea how to set about it.'

The Professor rose from his chair and stood with his back to the fire, looking down upon the young man. 'The trained mind,' he began oracularly, 'that is to say, the brain accustomed to logical reasoning processes, can often construct an edifice of unshakable truth from the loose bricks of fact which to others seem merely a profitless rubbish heap. I have studied the various incidents surrounding this case with particular care, firstly because I hoped you would come to me for advice, and secondly, because of the many points of interest they contain. As a result I may say that, if you will accept my assistance, there is a reasonable hope that together we may arrive at the solution of what is at present a mystery.'

Harold looked up sharply, with a look of incredulous wonder in his eyes. He had scarcely dared hope for even sympathy, and now here was this precise old mathematician not only sympathising, but actually offering his assistance to disperse the cloud that hung over him!

'Of course, sir, I'd be only too glad of your help,' he replied hesitatingly. 'But—'

The Professor cut him short. 'Then that's settled,' he said decisively. 'Now, the first thing is to marshal the facts as they are at present known to us. I may say that most of these are already in my possession. I have, as I have already informed you, followed the case with some attention. Perhaps the best method will be for me to state the facts as I know them. Should I be wrongly or inadequately informed, you will please supplement my knowledge.'

He relinquished his position by the mantelpiece, and lowered himself deliberately into his chair. A look of keen, almost hungry interest came into his eyes, the light of battle which always illumined him when he was engaged in wrestling with one of his favourite problems, especially if his solution promised to be at variance with that of the majority.

'When you had told your story at the police station, they sent for Inspector Hanslet, who was off duty,' he began abruptly. 'A constable was sent to Number 16, Riverside Gardens at once. On the arrival of Inspector Hanslet, and later the police surgeon, the three of you followed, and went straight to your bedroom, where the corpse was lying. Is that correct?'

'Quite, sir,' replied Harold. So much had been revealed at the inquest.

'Very well. Now to deal with the body itself. The result of examination showed it to be that of an elderly man, probably between fifty and sixty, clean-shaven, hair cut short—no easily identifiable distinguishing marks. He was apparently particular as to his personal appearance, his hair, which was turning grey, had recently been treated with some preparation designed to mask this greyness Against this, however, may be set the fact that his teeth had been neglected, and showed considerable signs of decay. His hands, on the contrary, were quite well kept, and bore no traces of manual labour.

'He was dressed in a remarkably tight-fitting blue serge suit, beneath which he wore underclothing bearing no laundry mark or trade description. This underclothing was distinctly light in texture for the time of year, a point to be noted in connection with the fact that he was apparently wearing no overcoat. The suit itself, though worn and far from new, was well-cut and probably made by an efficient tailor. It is particularly interesting, in view of the fact that the underclothing bore no marks of any kind, that this suit had been turned, turned inside out, that is to say, by an expert in these matters, and fitted with plain bone buttons. The man's boots were standard black-laced boots, of a well-known make. The most curious thing about them was that they were unusually tight-fitting, although worn over thin socks. No hat or cap of any kind was found.'

The Professor leaned back in his chair after the enumeration of these points, and looked keenly at Harold.

'Eliminating details, I think I have touched upon the essential facts connected with the man and his clothing,' he said. 'I deal with these first, as up to the present he remains unidentified, although, unlike the police, I consider the question of his identity of secondary importance. Now, so far as I have gone, have you anything to add?'

'Nothing, sir, except as regards the contents of his pockets,' replied Harold, who had been following the Professor's incisive words with keen attention.

'I am coming to that,' said the Professor. 'Do not let us confuse our classification of facts. From what we have seen so far, the police have deduced that the deceased was a non-manual worker, of limited means, compelled to maintain as decent an appearance as possible. In fact, a clerk of some kind or a burglar. Do you agree with this deduction?'

'I think so, sir,' replied Harold. 'But since you have put the facts as you have, it seems odd that all means of identification by the man's clothing were lacking. That hadn't struck me so forcibly before.'

'Humph!' grunted Professor Priestley. 'The usual failure to attach equal importance to every ascertainable fact, whether it appears relevant or not. I can hardly blame you, since this failing is common among men whom the world acclaims as trained scientists. But to continue. You spoke of the contents of the man's pockets. These were, I believe, as follows. A sum of one pound sixteen shillings and fourpence, made up of one pound and one ten-shilling note, two half-crowns, a shilling, three pennies, and two half-pennies, carried loose, that is to say, not in a purse or wallet. A nickelled steel tyre-lever, nine inches long, carried in the inside breast pocket, apparently quite new, and bearing the trade-mark of Motor Gadgets, Ltd., which is the steering-wheel of a motor-car. Besides this, half a dozen washers and nuts, showing various signs of wear, and odd parts of the valve of a motor-car tyre—these last all carried loose in the side pockets of the coat.

'Now observe once more that none of these things are of any assistance to identification. Treasury notes and coins are common currency, nobody dreams of noting the numbers of the notes which pass through his hands. Motor Gadgets, Ltd., are a big combine of manufacturers; this particular type of tyre lever is a standard article of theirs, and can be bought at any garage. Stray bolts, nuts, and parts of valves cannot, under ordinary circumstances, possibly be traced. You agree with me so far, I suppose?'

'Yes, sir,' replied Harold. 'There's just one thing about them, though. Taken together, they point to the man being in some way connected with motors in some form.'

'Thus to some extent controverting the clerk or burglar theory,' agreed the Professor. 'But a man who carries parts of a car about in his pockets is more likely to be a mechanic or chauffeur than a clerk in a garage, say. Now there are two points about this man which seem to render it unlikely that he had the actual handling of any machinery. The first is the state of his hands in general, and the fact that there was not the slightest trace of ingrained grime in the finer lines of his fingers in particular. That ingraining is remarkably persistent, as anyone who handles machinery will tell you. The second point is that there was no trace of oil or grease stains on his clothing. You may object that he never went near the machinery in the suit he was wearing when you found him. But still I maintain that oil particularly has a way of penetrating to the underclothing, and in this case the vest and drawers bore no signs of it.'

'How in the world do you know all this, sir?' exclaimed Harold in amazement. 'Nothing nearly so detailed came out at the inquest!'

Professor Priestley smiled indulgently. 'It seems that I have to some extent betrayed myself,' he replied. 'I had not meant to inform you of the fact at this stage, but Inspector Hanslet is a friend of mine. He is a man of very wide interests, as befits an officer charged with such important duties, and two or three years ago he happened to read a paper of mine on Methods of Psychological Deduction, in which, I venture to say, I succeeded in refuting some very widely-accepted theories. But no matter. Since that time he has often called upon me to ask my assistance in the correlation of scattered facts. I approached him three or four days ago, and he very willingly went over the case with me. He was very much interested in it then, although I expect that the verdict of the coroner's jury has now allayed his anxiety. I did not, of course, tell him that I was in any way interested in you.'

Harold gave a gasp of astonishment. The idea of this militant mathematician taking an interest in criminal cases was so novel that it seemed absurd. Mathematics was to him merely a jumble of queer signs and Greek letters; he had never considered it as a science applicable to human events.

'However,' continued the Professor, after a pause, 'that is by the way. The point I wish to make is that up to the present we have discovered nothing of great assistance towards establishing the identity of the deceased. We will now turn to a matter of even greater interest, and that is the cause of the man's death.

'You will remember that by your own statement the first thing that struck you was that the man's clothes were soaking with water. Investigation showed that the bed where he was lying was also very wet. The bed was in such a position that rain cannot have blown upon it from the window, and there was no sign of a leakage in the roof. Either, then, the man's clothes were soaked when they entered the room, or they were deliberately wetted after arrival. The fact that the carpet of the room showed signs of moisture is compatible with either theory. We must remember that, although there appears to be evidence of the source of the water, this evidence is not necessarily conclusive.'

'But surely,' interrupted Harold, 'the tracks leading up from the canal—'

The Professor held up a protesting hand. 'Let us wait until we come to that point,' he said. 'We are not at present considering how the body gained access to your rooms. Having established the condition of the corpse when found, that is, soaked with moisture and lying on its back on your bed, we come to the cause of death.

'Now, as a result of expert medical evidence, the coroner's jury returned a verdict of death from natural causes. A post-mortem had been held, and we must assume that the body had been very carefully examined, internally and externally, by experts familiar with the various methods by which life is terminated. It seems that these experts were able to rule out violence or poison as the cause of death. Now, I am no doctor, so I am compelled to rely upon the statements of others in this case. Until any fact appears to controvert this conclusion, we may accept it as probable.

'Examination of the body, however, revealed two salient facts. The first was that the left forearm bore minute marks—the number I have not been able to ascertain—such as might have been caused by a hypodermic syringe. From the position on the arm these marks might have been self-inflicted. The experts stated that the fact that no analytical or pathological traces of drugs could be discovered made it impossible that death could have been caused by some toxic injection. The second fact was that the deceased suffered from an affection of the heart of long standing, and of a nature which frequently terminates fatally. The existence of this heart affection caused one of the experts to put forward the suggestion that the marks on the forearm were the result of self-injection of some drug prescribed to relieve the heart, and that these injections had been made sufficiently long before death for all traces of the drug used to have vanished. I think that is a fair summary of the medical evidence?'

Harold nodded. He had learnt by now that interruptions of the Professor's train of thought were not welcome.

'Very well, then,' continued the Professor, 'you will agree, I think, that this evidence is mostly negative. Pressed to account for the fact that the man was dead and not alive when found, the medical witnesses—I say witnesses, for the police surgeon had sought the assistance of a Home Office expert—suggested that the deceased died of heart failure, brought on by sudden immersion on a cold night affecting an already-weakened organ. That the man died of heart failure was patent; I suppose most people die because the heart ceases to function for some cause or other. Whether this man's heart failed for the causes alleged, I cannot say. There may have been facts supporting the experts' view which are hidden from the mere lay mind. Were I to give an opinion, I should say it was a mere guess, although an extremely plausible one. In any case, the coroner and his jury seized upon it, and their verdict was the result.

'The next point of enquiry is obviously the time when the man died. The police surgeon, who saw the corpse at about five o'clock in the morning, expressed an opinion that the man had been dead not less than about nine or ten hours. Again, I have no knowledge or experience in such a matter, and we may provisionally accept this estimate as correct. In which case, the man may be assumed as having been dead by eight or nine o'clock the previous evening. According to your evidence you left your rooms at about four o'clock that evening, at which time, to your knowledge, the rooms contained no man, alive or dead.'

'That is so, sir,' replied Harold, seeing that the Professor paused, as though for confirmation. 'I fancy that the police had a vague suspicion that the body had been there all the time, since the doctors could only say that the man had been dead not less than eight or nine hours and not more than about twenty-four.'

'Possibly, possibly,' agreed the Professor. 'But certain other evidence, which, I confess, interests me far more than the question of the identity of the deceased, seemed to point in quite another direction. I mean the evidence concerning the means by which the corpse obtained access to your rooms. As you know, I have never visited Number 16, Riverside Gardens myself, but I received a description, an inadequate one, I admit, from a friend who has been there.'

'Inspector Hanslet again, sir?' suggested Harold.

'No,' replied the Professor. 'His mind was already made up. I wanted the description from someone who was unaware of the details which had been discovered. Evan Denbigh was able to supply me with the outline of what I required.'

'Denbigh!' exclaimed Harold, with some embarrassment. 'Oh yes, of course, he was there once, about six months ago. He came—'

Professor Priestley waited for the end of the sentence, but Harold had relapsed into silence.

'He told me why he went,' he said quietly. 'He was one of your friends who thought that you were making a fool of yourself. I fancy he went to see if you could not see reason.'

'Well, as a matter of fact, that's what he did come for,' agreed Harold. 'Jolly decent he was about it, too, really. He can't have seen much of the place, though. I was dressing for dinner, I had half my clothes flung about the sitting-room, and after he'd been there about ten minutes I went into the bedroom to wash and left him spouting to me through the door. He never saw the bedroom, where I found the body, at all.'

'So he told me,' replied the Professor. 'That is exactly why I want to see it for myself. Will you take me there, my boy?'

'Rather, sir!' exclaimed Harold. 'When would you like to go?'

Professor Priestley considered for a moment. 'I shall be disengaged at three o'clock tomorrow afternoon,' he replied. 'Now, my boy, I do not wish to raise your hopes unduly, but this case does not appear to me to be so hopeless as it seems. Good-bye until tomorrow.'

CHAPTER III

HAROLD returned to Riverside Gardens rather despondently. What he had expected as a result of his visit to Professor Priestley he hardly knew. It had been a sub-conscious impulse that had driven him to seek his father's old friend, an instinct to seek protection under the mantle of unquestioned respectability. His reception, contrary to what he had expected, had been warm, had somehow led him to expect an immediate dissipation of the clouds that had surrounded him. Whereas the result of their prolonged interview seemed to leave the matter exactly where it had stood before.

Remember, Harold's desire to solve the mystery was very keen. He had been through a remarkably unpleasant ordeal, had been an object of strong suspicion, and had been put through a very fine mill of inquisition. He had come out of it with hardly a shred of decency left to him; the papers had published full reports of the inquest, at which he had figured in none too favourable a light. And, worst of all, although the verdict had exonerated him from the accusation of having caused the man's death, he was conscious that there was a pretty strong notion abroad that he knew more about the business than he had divulged.

He felt like an outlaw, shunned by the whole world. Return to his former life was impossible; the Naxos Club had been raided and dispersed, notoriously as the result of his enforced account of his doings on that fatal evening, and he could scarcely expect his old friends to welcome him with open arms. A return to the world of respectability was impossible while the stigma of intangible wrong-doing still attached to him. The only way out that he could see was to discover the truth of the mysterious circumstances that had involved him in their toils. Professor

Priestley had led him to believe that this was possible, and had left him with nothing more cheering than that the business was not so hopeless as it looked!

The first thing Harold noticed as he opened the gate of Number 16, Riverside Gardens, was that the door of Mr Boost's shop was open. As he came up the path the proprietor himself came out and barred his further passage, silent, accusing.

'Good evening, Mr Boost,' said Harold politely. 'So you're back again?'

The man made no reply, but stood looking at him malevolently. He was tall and thin, with a pronounced stoop, sharply-cut features and a curiously intense look in his eyes. He wore an untidy-looking tweed suit but the most striking thing about him was an enormous red scarf, which did duty both as a collar and tie, and an equally pretentious red handkerchief, a good half of which protruded from the side pocket of his coat. He was obviously not the sort of person to disguise his political convictions.

This individual regarded Harold for some moments in silence. Then he suddenly turned and led the way into the shop, beckoning to Harold to follow him. He closed the door behind them, then, for the first time, spoke.

'What did you do it for, comrade?' he asked, in a surprisingly deep voice, that seemed to come from some strange vocal organs concealed within his narrow chest.

Harold turned upon him indignantly. 'What the devil do you mean?' he replied angrily. 'You seem to know all about it. Haven't you heard that the police found that I had nothing to do with it? I shouldn't wonder if you knew more about it than I do.'

'Damn the police!' exclaimed Mr Boost. 'They're only the servants of a tyrannical capitalism. The first thing we shall do will be to discard them and set up Red Guards who'll know their business instead. Police, indeed! Why, they had the sauce to come to me in Leicester where I was doing a lot of business and badger the life out of me. Where was I that night? Did I know the man who had been found dead in my house? Showed me his photograph and description and cross-questioned me till I told them what I thought of them. I wouldn't give a curse for anything the police might think.'

Harold smiled. He recalled a remark of Inspector Hanslet. 'Boost? Oh, yes, we know all about him. He's harmless enough, but we'll have him looked up, though, for all that.' But he refrained from repeating it to his landlord.

'What your idea was I don't know and I don't want to know,' continued Mr Boost. 'You seem to have scrambled out of it, and I suppose that's all you care about. But you can't expect me to thank you for bringing every silly fool in London to gape round this place. I thought you wanted to lie low when you came here.'

He went into the back room, still grumbling, and Harold, seeing the futility of trying to persuade him of his innocence, took the opportunity of going up to his own rooms. He spent the evening trying to write, and then at last, giving up the task in despair, went to bed and slept fitfully, dreaming impossible dreams in which the dead man, Boost, Professor Priestley and a host of minor characters came and went, mocking him, scorning him for the outcast he was.

At nine o'clock Mrs Clapton, from Number 15 over the way, thundered at his door, as was her custom. When he had first come to Riverside Gardens he had engaged her to come in for an hour every morning to tidy the place up. The Paddington Mystery, as the headlines had called it, had raised her to the seventh heaven of delight. In an incautious moment Inspector Hanslet had called upon her to ask a few questions, and had only succeeded in escaping after an hour of breathless volubility which had left his head in an aching whirl. Since that moment she had regaled her neighbours and all whom she could prevail upon to listen to her with a torrent of eloquence. As the only person besides the central figure who had access to the scene of the discovery, she poured forth in an unceasing stream the little she knew and the enormous volume of what she conjectured.

But this morning Harold was in no mood to listen to her theories or her remarkably frank comments. He put on a dressing-gown and let her in, then returned again to bed, leaving her the run of the sitting-room. For her regulation hour she busied herself in moving the furniture about, then, after making several unsuccessful attempts to engage Harold in conversation through the closed door, she departed, firmly convinced that her employer had something discreditable to conceal. 'It's hawful the life that young man leads,' she was wont to whisper. 'I've seen him go in with girls after dark—you mark my words, there's somethink be'ind it all!'

Harold waited for the door to bang behind her, then wearily made up his mind to get up. He was half dressed, when once more a loud and insistent knocking on the door disturbed his train of thought.

With a muttered imprecation he went down stairs, to find Boost standing on his doorstep.

Harold frowned. He and his landlord had always got on pretty well hitherto. Boost had never abandoned the hope of converting his tenant to the doctrines of Communism, and had called upon him at all sorts of hours for that purpose. The man's energy and ferocity had amused him; he had regarded him as a harmless crank whose proper field of action was surely Soviet Russia. But now he had other things to think of, and was in no mood for a lecture upon the iniquities of the bourgeois and the advantages of the Dictatorship of the Proletariat.

'Good morning, Mr Boost,' he said coldly. 'What can I do for you? I'm going out as soon as I've finished dressing.'

'You and I've got to have a word first,' replied Mr Boost truculently. 'There's a question or two to which I want an answer.'

Harold shrugged his shoulders and led the way upstairs. He might as well hear what the man had to say and get it over.

Mr Boost settled himself in Harold's best chair and plunged into his subject without delay. 'Look here!' he said sharply. 'I want to know what your game was the other night.'

Harold sighed wearily. 'Oh, Lord, you know all about that!' he exclaimed. 'I suppose you read the papers?'

'Yes, I read them right enough,' replied Mr Boost. 'I don't want to pry into your affairs so long as they don't concern me. When they do, I'm going to have the truth. What happened to my bale of goods, I'd like to know?'

Harold stared at him in amazement. 'Your bale of goods?' he repeated. 'What the devil are you talking about? What bale of goods?'

Mr Boost regarded him suspiciously. 'I reckon you know more about it than I do,' he said. 'Especially as it happens I've never seen it.'

'Look here, Mr Boost. I don't know what the hell you're talking about,' replied Harold, now thoroughly roused. 'I haven't got anything of yours, you can search the place if you like. And when you've finished I'll trouble you to clear out and leave me in peace.'

Mr Boost laughed scornfully. 'Oh, I don't suppose you've got it here,' he said. 'But it's like this. I'm not such a fool as to believe that a man comes and dies in these rooms without your knowing something about it. And when a bale of goods of mine disappears on the same night, I can't help thinking that you know something about that, too.'

'How do you know it disappeared that night?' enquired Harold sharply.

'Did you see it leaning up against my door under the porch when you came home that night?' replied Mr Boost aggressively. 'Or were you too beastly drunk to notice anything?'

Harold paused a moment. 'I won't swear about when I first came in,' he said. 'It was nearly pitch dark, you know. But I know jolly well that there was nothing there when I came back with the police. Someone would have seen it if there had been. And there wasn't anything there when I went out that evening.'

'Of course there wasn't,' replied Mr Boost testily. 'It hadn't been delivered then. Well, I'll have to tell you what happened, I suppose. You get my stuff back from your pals, and I won't ask any questions. That's fair.'

Harold started to make an indignant refutation, but Mr Boost silenced him.

'Now, just you listen,' he interrupted. 'I've got some stuff coming down from Leicester, and I've just been up to see George, who keeps a van up along the Harrow Road and does a bit of carting for me now and then. I've fixed up with him to fetch this stuff from the station, and when I was leaving him he says, "Did you find that lot all right I left for you the other evening, Mr Boost?"'

'"What other evening?" I said. "You haven't done a job for me for the last couple of months, George!"'

'"Why, the evening before that there body was found in your house, Mr Boost," he said. "That's how I remember the evening it was. I must have been along at your place about an hour or so before the chap broke in."'

'Well, I knew of nothing coming while I was away, though it does sometimes happen that a friend of mine in the trade sends something along which he knows I can do with. Very often the carman, if he knows me, leaves the stuff outside the door. It's safe enough in the front garden, especially if it's heavy, as it usually is. You've seen stuff standing under the porch before now, haven't you?'

Harold nodded. 'Yes, but I've seen nothing there while you've been away,' he said.

Mr Boost looked at him suspiciously. 'Well, it wasn't there when I came back, and so I told George. "What was it, anyhow, and where did it come from?" I asked him.

'"I don't know what it was, but it was middling heavy," he

said. "I got a message from old Samuels that he had some stuff for you, and I was to be particular and fetch it that very evening. So down I went to Camberwell, picked up the stuff about four, and was back with it here between five and six."

'Well, I didn't know of anything old Samuels had for me, but there was nothing in that. He's a comrade, or he used to be, he's got a bit slack lately. Calls himself Samuels, but his real name's Szamuelly. One of his relations was one of Lenin's men, and fought a glorious fight for the cause in Hungary. Killed himself rather than be caught when the capitalists put the bourgeois back again. Never mind, that won't last long. The whole of Europe is already on the brink—'

'But this man Samuels and his bale of goods?' interrupted Harold, feeling that an account of anything that happened on that fatal evening was preferable to an oration on Bolshevism.

Mr Boost checked himself and returned to his story. 'Well, George told me that he got the message—there's a telephone belonging to a man in his yard, and he'll take a message for George from one of us dealers—and went down to Samuels' place. He didn't see the old man himself, but heard him wheezing and coughing in the back shop. When George raps on the counter, out comes Samuels' nephew, a half-witted sort of chap who comes and lives with his uncle when he can't get a job anywhere else. The nephew shows him a bale done up with mats and rope, and between them they got it into the van. George says it was about six foot long, and weighed best part of a couple of hundredweight. "Uncle says if Mr Boost isn't in, you can leave it under the porch, it won't hurt in the open for a night or two," the nephew tells him. George asks if he can have his money, twelve-and-six, for the job. The nephew goes into the back room, and George hears the old man coughing and wheezing again. I'll bet he did, too.'

Mr Boost allowed his austere frown to melt into a smile at the idea. 'Old Samuels is worth a lot of money,' he explained, 'but it's like drawing a tooth to get a shilling out of him. By and by the nephew comes back, and gives George his twelve-and-sixpence exact, not a penny more for a drink, you may bet. George comes straight here, or so he says, carries the stuff up to the door, and props it under the porch. And what I want to know is, what's become of it?'

Mr Boost fixed his fiery eye upon Harold, as though he expected him to confess immediately to the theft of this bale of goods. But for a moment Harold made no reply. There seemed no reason to doubt the truth of the story—in any case it could easily be verified by referring to George or to Mr Boost's friend, old Samuels. It was just possible that the disappearance of this bale was in some way connected with the other mysterious happening of that eventful night.

'Look here, Mr Boost,' he said at last. 'I may be a pretty fair rotter, but at least I haven't tried my hand at theft, as yet. Besides, if I wanted to steal a bale of that size and weight, I shouldn't know how to set about it or where to dispose of it. For that matter, I can account for every minute of my time that evening. I give you my word I know nothing of the matter. Will that do?'

Mr Boost's frown relaxed a little. 'I'm not saying you took it,' he conceded. 'But there were some pretty queer happenings about here that night, and I reckon that you know more about them than you're prepared to say. How do I know that the disappearance of that bale hasn't got something to do with them?'

'Well, Mr Boost, I can only assure you that nobody wants to know what happened that night more than I do,' replied Harold. Then he added maliciously, 'Why don't you tell the police about it? They'd be glad to help you, I dare say.'

'Police!' exclaimed Mr Boost contemptuously. 'I don't want them fooling about with my business. I don't recognise their right to interfere in a free man's affairs. No, I'm going to find out about this myself, I am.'

'In that case, I shall be very pleased to give you all the help I can,' replied Harold. 'I have an idea if we could find out what happened to your bale of goods, we should learn something about the man I found dead in my bed. What was in this precious bale, anyhow?'

Mr Boost shook his head. 'I don't know,' he said. 'Old Samuels' nephew didn't tell George. Don't suppose he knew; the old man keeps his business pretty much to himself. He knew I should find out what it was when I opened it, and that was good enough for him.'

'Was it likely to have been anything of any great value?' suggested Harold.

'Old Samuels wouldn't have told George to leave it in the porch if it had been. Besides, he'd have written to me by now asking for the money. He doesn't like parting with anything that's worth much, doesn't that old man.'

'Then the only way to find out what was in the bale is to ask old Samuels himself,' said Harold. 'Why don't you write him a note and find out? You can't begin to trace the stuff until you know what it was.'

Mr Boost shook his head. 'No, I don't care to write,' he replied. 'Like as not the old man wouldn't answer, or if he did, would send a bill for the stuff. And I can't very well go and see him today, I don't want to leave the place till George has delivered that lot from Leicester.'

An idea struck Harold and he blurted it out before he had time to consider the consequences it might entail.

'Look here, Mr Boost, I'm as interested in the fate of this bale of goods as you are, only for a slightly different reason. Someone must have taken it away that night, and it is just possible that that someone could throw some light on what I want to know. If you like, I'll go to Camberwell and see old Samuels for you.'

Mr Boost considered for a moment without replying. 'Couldn't do no harm,' he said at last, rather reluctantly. 'If you can get anything at all out of the old man, that is. He's as close as an oyster. I'm beginning to believe that your story's right, that you've been fooled over this night's business same as I have. Perhaps that fellow did break in after my stuff. But if so, what did he take the trouble to climb up to your rooms for? Why break in if the stuff he wanted was already outside? How did he get it away if he was dead? No, it beats me, but it may not be your fault, after all. Yes, you can go and see old Samuels, if you like.'

'Thank you, Mr Boost, I will,' replied Harold gravely. 'What sort of a chap is the old man, anyway?'

'He's a queer old fish,' replied Mr Boost. 'Always grumbling and grousing under his breath. You can't tell what he's saying, he mumbles so. To look at him, you wouldn't think he had a bean in the world, though I know for a fact he's got some thousands locked up in a tin box in the back room. He doesn't know I know that, or I believe he'd murder me. He's a stingy old skinflint as ever you've heard of; I've only known him wear one suit of clothes all the time I've known him, all loose and baggy, with about half a dozen ragged waistcoats underneath it. You can hardly see his face, he's all shaggy like a bear, long hair, whiskers and beard, which haven't ever been combed, by the look of it. Like as not, unless you tell him you come from me, he'll mumble and cough at you and tell you to mind your own business.'

'I'll risk that,' said Harold with a smile. 'I'll be off to see old Samuels or Szamuelly tomorrow afternoon. What's his address, by the way?'

'Thirty-six, Inkerman Street, Camberwell,' replied Mr Boost. 'A tram from Victoria will take you pretty close to the place. It's a little shop up a side street, not unlike this, only he's more stuff in his window. He does a bit of retail trade sometimes.'

'All right, I'll find it,' said Harold. 'Any message for him?'

'No, I don't think he wants my love,' said Mr Boost sourly. 'You may not find him in, he goes about the country buying sometimes, same as I do. I rather thought he'd be in Leicester the other day. Don't you go and tell him I lost that stuff, if you see him.'

'Not I,' replied Harold. 'You can rely on me to tell him no more than I can help.'

Mr Boost nodded and left the room. Harold, remembering his appointment with Professor Priestley, got through the intervening time as best he could, and was shown into the Professor's study punctually at three o'clock.

CHAPTER IV

'WE will take a taxi-cab,' said the Professor as soon as they were outside the house. 'I should like to approach Riverside Gardens in the same way as you approached it that night.'

So it happened that Professor Priestley and Harold were set down at the Register Office, and walked through the side streets to Mr Boost's house. They were regarded with interest by the few inhabitants of the neighbourhood they met on their way; the case had attracted considerable attention in the newspapers, and the locality had for some days been a centre of pilgrimage. Harold shrank from the interested scrutiny and scarcely-veiled personal remarks, but the Professor's attention seemed wholly devoted to close observation of his surroundings.

The first remark made by the latter was evoked by the spectacle of Mr Boost's front garden. It was certainly a deplorable sight, littered with broken wooden crates, straw, shavings, and the remnants of the woven mats employed by furniture packers, with here and there a broken-down piece of furniture among the jumble.

'This antique dealer of yours seems to be a slovenly sort of person,' commented the Professor. 'He lives in a room leading from the shop, I believe?'

'Yes, when he is here,' replied Harold. 'He's very often away, attending sales in the country. It is a pity that he was not at home when all this happened. He would have been bound to see the man break in.'

'Humph. Is he here now?' asked the Professor.

'Not to my knowledge, sir,' replied Harold. 'I don't think he can have come back, by the look of the place. He's a queer sort of fellow, a raging Communist, according to his own account. He comes and goes without a word to me, though when he's here he sometimes stops me for a chat.'

34

'What happens to the shop in his absence?' asked the Professor.

'It isn't exactly a shop in the sense that people come and buy things at it,' replied Harold. 'It's more a sort of a warehouse. Now and then a van comes and either brings or takes away a lot of stuff. I don't know where it comes from or whom it goes to.'

'I should like to meet Mr Boost,' said the Professor reflectively. 'Now, I do not think we need remain here. Perhaps you will lead the way upstairs into your own rooms.'

Harold took him upstairs, through the sitting-room, at which he cast but a cursory glance, and into the bedroom.

'Nothing has been moved since the events of the other night?' asked the Professor. 'The bed, and so forth, occupy the same relative positions?'

'Exactly the same,' replied Harold.

'Very well,' said the Professor. 'Now describe to me exactly how you found the body.'

Harold complied with this request as well as he was able. When he had finished, the Professor walked to the window, and stood looking out of it in silence.

It was not a very cheerful prospect. Immediately below the window sill was a sloping corrugated-iron roof, terminating in a drop of about six feet into a paved courtyard. This courtyard was even more unkempt than the front garden, ankle deep in sodden straw and littered with packing cases of all shapes and sizes. It was bounded on three sides by a five-foot brick wall, the fourth being the back of the house. Beyond the wall on the side furthest from the house was a waste patch of land, about a quarter of an acre in extent, and beyond this again a small patch of garden belonging to a public house, which had a door opening on to this garden. Beyond the wall on the left side of the courtyard was the canal, its filthy water lapping the wall itself, since the towing-path was on the further bank. Beyond the wall on the right was the exactly similar courtyard of Number 14, Riverside Gardens. Looking straight out of the window, the most conspicuous object was an ugly massive-looking bridge, by which Great Western Road crossed the canal, about a hundred yards distant.

The Professor turned from the window after a prolonged inspection. 'I see, I see, *most* interesting,' he muttered. 'Now, abandoning facts for the moment, let us return to the discoveries of the police on their arrival.

'The first thing they noticed, I understand, was that this window had been forced. I notice that the hasp is still loose. I infer that nothing has been done to it since that night?'

'Nothing whatever, sir,' replied Harold. 'Everything has been left exactly as it was found.'

The Professor put on his glasses, and gazed at the hasp as though it were a term in some indeterminate equation. Two screws still held it loosely to the window-frame, and with these he played absently while he continued his interrogation.

'Excellent,' he commented. 'And outside the window the police found marks showing how the window had been forced?'

Harold lifted the lower half of the window and pointed to slight indentations on the bottom of the sash and on the window-frame. 'You can see the marks where he inserted the tyre-lever, in order to force the window up from the outside,' he said. 'The lever found in his pocket exactly fitted these marks, and fragments of paint from the window-frame were found on the end of it.'

'So I understand,' said the Professor. 'The next clue was a track of regular footprints leading from a point on the canal bank about the middle of that waste land to the foot of the wall at the end of the courtyard. The police having removed the boots found on the corpse, discovered that they exactly fitted those footprints, and that the length of the stride was such as might have been expected from a man of the deceased's stature.'

'That's right, sir,' put in Harold, imagining from the Professor's silence that he expected some reply. 'Inspector Hanslet was highly delighted—'

But the Professor waved him to silence. 'Inspector Hanslet

has, naturally, no doubt as to the sequence of events,' he said. 'There were, I understand, footsteps on the opposite bank of the canal, which appear to indicate that the deceased gained access to the towing-path from Great Western Road. We will walk round and look at the place where these were found later. For the present I think we are in possession of all the facts discovered by the police?'

'So far as I know, we are,' agreed Harold.

'Very well then. You know my methods. Recognise facts when you see them, and construct your hypotheses only from their aid. What is your theory regarding the movements of the man during the twelve hours preceding your discovery of his body?'

Harold hesitated. It seemed to him that all this was a waste of time, that Professor Priestley, with his love of facts, his passion for logical deduction, must see the official story was the only possible one. At all events, Harold, for his part, had no alternative to offer.

'It seems simple enough,' he replied, 'although I admit it is very strange that the man should choose a place like this to break into. Perhaps he meant to ransack Boost's shop below.'

'Never mind the motive,' said the Professor sharply. 'Tell me what you think happened that night.'

'Well, I imagine that this man, whoever he was, set out with the intention of breaking in somewhere. Unless he had completely lost himself in the fog, and mistook this house for an entirely different one, we must assume that this was his objective, since his tracks led straight here. He forced an entry with a tool he carried for the purpose, and then, overcome by his efforts, and by his soaking on a cold night—for both his tracks and the state of his clothes show that he swam the canal— he found his heart failing him and just lay down on the bed and died.'

'A most inconsiderate thing to do in a total stranger's house,' commented the Professor drily. And then his tone changed suddenly, and he looked fixedly at Harold from behind his glasses.

'If you want my help in this, my boy, you must tell me the whole truth,' he said quietly. 'Is it a fact that this man was a complete stranger to you? Can you think of no one answering to his description who would have any reason for entering your rooms for any purpose?'

'I assure you, sir, that I haven't the remotest idea who he could be,' replied Harold frankly. 'Heaven knows I've been cudgelling my brains ever since to find some motive for the fellow breaking in here. There's nothing of value that he could take away.'

'I gather from your evidence that you missed nothing?' enquired the Professor.

'Nothing at all, sir. The police made me go over everything two or three times.'

The Professor smiled rather grimly. 'I rather sympathise with Inspector Hanslet,' he said. 'The case appealed to him, I know, and since the verdict deprived him of the excuse of murder or even manslaughter, he tried hard to find burglary to justify the continuance of his investigations. Well, my boy, I believe you as to the man being a total stranger to you. That is a fact which at present seems to indicate that we must approach the solution of the mystery from other directions than that of motive.'

'Surely, sir, the easiest line of investigation is through the man's identity,' ventured Harold. 'We know he died in these rooms about eight o'clock on that evening—'

'How do we know that?' interrupted the Professor sharply.

'It cannot have been later, according to the doctors, and it cannot have been much earlier, or he would surely have been seen as he swam the canal and crossed the waste land, even on a foggy evening. There's always somebody about quite as late as that. It seems very odd that he wasn't seen, as it is.'

'Well, postulating for the moment that the man died in these rooms about eight o'clock that evening, what then?'

'Why, sir, he must have come from somewhere, must have friends or acquaintances of some sort. It amazes me that after all the publicity the case has had, the body lying in the mortuary, and all that, somebody hasn't come forward who knew him. He must have been missing from somewhere for a week now. Sooner or later, it will be discovered that somebody answering his description is missing, and then we shall know who he was. Once we know that, the mystery will be solved.'

'I wonder!' said the Professor, with the ghost of a smile. 'I cannot allow that your reasoning is logical. You infer that knowledge of his identity would result in discovery of the reasons why you found him here. This is not necessarily so. But you touch upon one very interesting matter, the question of disappearance without attracting attention. I have frequently speculated upon this very point. It is one of the results of civilisation that every unit of mankind is to a greater or less extent involved with his fellow units, and cannot vanish without the knowledge of others. It is, as you suggest, curious that any human being should disappear from his accustomed environment, as you assume that this man has done, and that, in spite of the widest publicity, of the publication of photographs and descriptions, there should exist no one who could associate the disappearance with the discovery. In this case particularly, of a decently-dressed man with money in his pocket the possibility is even more remote.'

'That is exactly what I cannot understand, sir,' replied Harold eagerly. 'It seems to me that it must be possible to find someone who knew him.'

'But how?' interrupted the Professor swiftly. 'If he or she has not yet been found, do you think your efforts are likely to be successful? Look at the facts. They point to one thing, to collusion. When you find out who this man was, you will also discover that someone knew of his disappearance. Nor should I be surprised if that someone knew that the corpse was here long before even you did. No, my boy, the line upon which to seek the solution of the mystery lies in another direction from the question of identity. To my mind, the first thing to discover is how the corpse reached the position in which you found it.'

'But surely, sir, that's obvious!' exclaimed Harold. 'The tracks across the waste land, made beyond question by the dead man, the forced window—'

The Professor rose abruptly from his chair. 'Of course, of course!' he said. 'Facts are incontrovertible, the only thing needful is to recognise them when you see them. Now, before it gets dark, I should like to see the place where the footmarks were found on the other side of the canal.'

The two left the house, and in a few minutes were standing on the bridge crossing the canal. A steady stream of vehicles and foot-passengers passed them as they leaned over the parapet, a barge laden with timber floated lazily eastwards, drawn by a sleepy-looking horse, its passage producing oily-looking ripples in the black water.

From where they stood, the backs of Numbers 2 to 16, Riverside Gardens were clearly visible in the last of the daylight. The public-house was not yet open, but a group of children were playing at one end of the waste land, and at the other an elderly man was digging hopefully, as though he proposed to convert its barrenness into an allotment. It was perfectly obvious that nobody could perform the feat of swimming the canal and climbing up to Harold's window during the hours of daylight without attracting attention.

'You see how public the place is, sir,' said Harold. 'Even after dark, at all events until closing time, the windows of that public-house shine right over the waste land. Yet the fellow must have broken in before ten o'clock. It was only the fog that prevented his being seen.'

The Professor made no reply. He walked slowly to the northern end of the bridge, until he stood directly over the towing-path. On his right was a brick wall, against which, some ten yards from the bridge, stood a telegraph pole, its base buried in the side of the towing-path nearest to the wall.

'His footmarks were found at the bottom of that pole,' volunteered Harold. 'It seems pretty obvious what happened. There are no means of getting on to the towing-path from the road, except through a door in that wall, which is always kept locked. It seems that the man tried this door first; there happens to be a sand-heap close to it on the outside, and Inspector Hanslet found an impression of his boot there too. Then, as he couldn't open it, he must have come back to where we're standing, waited till there was no one about, then clambered along the top of the wall till he reached the telegraph pole. All he had to do then was to swarm down it—you see there are brackets on it part of the way down—and he was on the towing-path. Then he swam across, landed on the opposite bank—the footsteps on the waste land began about opposite the telegraph pole—and the rest was easy.'

The Professor nodded, and Harold was emboldened to continue.

'If he'd waited till after ten, he would have saved himself a lot of trouble. He could have climbed over the opposite end of the bridge into the garden of the public-house. He would have run just as little danger of being seen with the fog as thick as it was. I can't think why he didn't.'

But the Professor appeared to be paying no attention to him. He was staring at the window of Harold's room with a frown on his face, as though he suspected it of responsibility in the matter. Suddenly he took his watch from his pocket and glanced at it impatiently.

'Dear me!' he exclaimed. 'It is later than I thought. I have spent a most interesting afternoon.'

Then suddenly he put his hand on Harold's shoulder. 'Do not allow yourself to take this matter too much to heart, my boy,' he said kindly. 'Come and see me again in a day or two. I must have time to think. Where can I find a taxi-cab to take me home?'

CHAPTER V

On the following afternoon Harold, true to his promise made to Mr Boost, set out to interview Mr Samuels. During his tedious journey to Camberwell he had plenty of time for thought. His fit of despondency was by no means at an end; he still felt the crushing burden of the unsolved mystery in which he had become entangled, and, writhe as he might, could find no means of divesting himself of it. Professor Priestley had indeed put out a hand to lighten it, but his efforts had not been crowned with any very conspicuous success. He felt himself an outcast in the ways of the noisy city which clamoured about him; friendless, furtive, dreading to see a look of recognition in every face that glanced at him, dreading to overhear the hoarse whisper, 'Look, mate, that's the bloke whose house they found the corpse in!'

Friendless, yes. All that gay crowd who knew him as 'Merry Devil' at the Naxos, they, most of them, sailed too near the wind themselves to care for the contact of one upon whom the shadow of suspicion still rested. Besides, that wretched business of the raiding of the place was scarcely calculated to increase his popularity. Not that he cared; they could go. The shock he had experienced had determined him to keep clear of that crowd in future. To his not over-logical reasoning the thing that had happened to him appeared as a judgment on his habits. If he hadn't been in the habit of going out all night, of coming home drunk, he might—oh, damn!

No, all that crowd could go for all he cared. Yet—it was queer that Vere had made no sign all this time. He had last seen her about a couple of days before that fatal evening, and they had arranged to meet at the Naxos as usual. Since then, ten days ago now, he had heard no word of her. Why had she not turned up as she had promised? That question still puzzled him. As for the reason of her silence since, that had been plain enough. Vere, whose days were spent in the lap of respectability as the principal clerk of the Women's Social League, was far too careful to take any step which would openly endanger her reputation. She was one more friend gone, that was all. Still, Vere, after all that had happened between them—

Of the rest, whom could he count upon? There were one or two fellows he had known, but they had somehow drifted out of his life, and he scarcely knew their whereabouts, even had he felt inclined to inflict himself upon them. After all, very few people exactly welcome a visit from the man who has furnished notorious copy for the sensation-loving Press. Apart from these, there remained only Professor Priestley and his daughter, and Evan Denbigh. The Professor had behaved like a brick, but he had not suggested that Harold and April should meet again. As for Denbigh—well, the last time he had come to see him his reception had not been so cordial as to encourage a further advance on his part. No, it was not to be expected that Denbigh would seek him out.

Harold found himself comparing himself with this man, about his own age, but his very opposite in character and attainments. He was the son of poor parents, born somewhere in Wales, by his own account, in a little village with an unpronounceable name. He had come to town to try his fortune, and through sheer hard work had secured a medical degree. In the course of his training he had attracted the attention of Sir Alured Faversham, the world-renowned pathologist, and had been adopted by him as his principal assistant. As Denbigh himself said modestly, it was not an extraordinarily remunerative job, but it gave him more than enough to live on, and opened up all sorts of possibilities. A young man so closely associated with Sir Alured was not likely to want opportunities.

Professor Priestley had met this promising scholar at Sir Alured's house, and had been greatly taken by him. It may be supposed that his mind, working always upon logical lines, had determined that here was a desirable husband for April, Harold having so obviously failed to develop along the lines of his early promise. April, on her part, had thrown no obstacles in the path. She was, as she herself expressed it, fed up with Harold and his methods. Not that she was shocked—such an attitude would have been impossible to a girl of her generation. But—well, there are limits, and Harold had clearly overstepped them. Besides, he seemed to prefer other company to her own, and, so long as that was the case, she could hardly have been expected to trouble her head about him. Evan, on the other hand, was good-looking, attentive, devoted, always eager to take her out to dinner, dance or show. The alluring intimacy of the returning taxi never tempted him beyond the bounds of propriety. They were not engaged; nothing of the kind had even been suggested. But it would not occasion any widespread surprise if they were to become so. Harold, contemplating the possibility, felt a much keener stab than his don't-care attitude, his entanglement with Vere, gave him any right to expect.

The tram, into which he had changed at Victoria, as Mr Boost had directed him, crawled along with much clanging of its insistent bell, and at last Harold, awakening from his reverie, realised that he had reached Camberwell. He got out of the vehicle, and began to make enquiries as to the whereabouts of Inkerman Street. He found it, not without some difficulty, for it seemed to lie some little distance off the tram and bus routes. Turning into it from a long street of mean houses, he noticed a public-house at the corner, and an untidy litter of paper and orange-peel stretching before him. A few loud-voiced children were playing in the roadway, and an iron-shod lorry, laden with bars of iron, progressed over the irregular asphalt with a deafening clatter. Harold waited till it was out of earshot, then turned the corner and followed it.

Inkerman Street had obviously been designed by its optimistic builder as a residential neighbourhood of the middle class. Its houses, though probably jerry-built, had at one time worn the stucco of respectability, and might have attracted the careful minds of conscientious clerks with inconveniently large families. But if such tenants had ever inhabited these rather featureless houses, they had departed long ago, and the neighbourhood had fallen from its early promise. Most of the stucco had peeled off, leaving ugly scars of dirty brickwork; the landlords, deriving what income they could from letting off rooms to the poorest classes, had very little left to spend on paint. Inkerman Street was, in fact, a slum, a district which had fallen upon evil days, and the tokens of its former respectability served only to emphasise its downfall.

Some of the houses had been converted into shops, most of which dealt in sweets, tobacco, and queer-looking picture papers with unfamiliar titles. Harold noticed a combined baker and milkman, through the open door of which he could read the staring and ominous words of a prominent notice: 'Please do not ask for credit, as a refusal often offends.' Here and there, at the open door of one of the houses, stood a slatternly woman, calling shrilly to Alf or Ivy, threatening them with unheard-of penalties for incomprehensible misdeeds.

Riverside Gardens was Mayfair compared with this, but Harold had no qualms where slums were concerned. He walked slowly down the dirty pavement, looking for Number 36. It proved to be one of the largest houses in the street, and was peculiar from the fact that its door was shut. The windows were uncurtained, and were covered with the grime of ages, but it was just possible to discern through them that the rooms were full of heavy tattered furniture and rubbish of all descriptions, piled up in the utmost disorder. Harold smiled; the place was an exact replica of Mr Boost's shop; larger, certainly, but filled with the same curious and apparently valueless merchandise.

Printed above the shop in bold letters was the name Isaac Samuels, but Harold hardly needed to glance at this. He had obviously reached the place he sought; the owner of all this trash was the very man to have dealings with Mr Boost. He mounted a couple of steps, tried the door, and found it locked. An old and rusty knocker hung precariously close to his hand, and with this he rapped smartly and waited. The noisy life of the street surged round him disinterestedly, and he could hear no sound from within above its clamour. He knocked again, more violently, and a man, unshaven and in his shirt-sleeves, appeared at the door of one of the houses opposite and cast a reflective eye upon him. As Harold knocked for the third time, the man took his pipe from his mouth, spat on the pavement, and called across the road. ''Tain't no good knockin' on that door, mister,' he said.

Harold desisted from his attempts, and, seeing that his informant still stood watching him, crossed the street and walked up to him.

'Isn't Mr Samuels at home?' he enquired.

The man spat again, turned the question over in his mind, and then replied slowly. 'Oh, yes, he's at home all right,' he said. 'But 'e don't answer no knocks, an' if yer wants anything from 'im, that's not the way ter go about it.'

'But how am I to get in without knocking?' enquired Harold.

'You can't,' replied the man conclusively.

'Well, I've got a message for him from a friend of his,' persevered Harold, aware that an explanation of his own business was the only way of gaining any information. 'How am I to give it to him if I can't get in?'

'Ah! That's the rub,' said the man in shirt-sleeves, with a frown of consideration. 'Old Samuels, 'e won't open the door, never mind how hard you knock. Ill in bed, 'e is, and 'e won't thank you for disturbing of 'im, neither. Why, I ain't seen 'im myself for over a week. 'Eard 'im, though, 'eard 'im cough and swear at that young nevvy of 'is, young Isidore. Best write a note and slip it under the door. Isidore 'll find it when 'e comes home.'

Harold considered a moment. 'Isidore's out, I take it?' he suggested.

"Course 'e is,' replied the man. "E don't come 'ome till after five, and if anyone's got business with Samuels, they've got to wait till 'e opens up the place then. So now you know.'

A door opened somewhere in the house behind them, and a shrill voice was heard declaiming with the utmost volubility. 'That's the missus,' said the man, as he turned on his heel. 'Best thing you can do is to wait for the nevvy,' and with that he disappeared.

Harold made up his mind that since he had come so far he had better wait for the 'nevvy.' After all, according to Mr Boost's account, it was this young man who had delivered the bale of goods to George, so that he might be expected to know the nature of its contents. Besides, Harold was by no means sorry at the chance of escaping from an interview with the formidable Mr Samuels. There was more than a likelihood that that worthy would tell him to go away and mind his own business.

He looked at his watch, and found that it was already past four o'clock. The 'nevvy' was reputed to come home after five, so that he had about an hour in front of him. He strolled along to the end of Inkerman Street, and found it led to a very similar thoroughfare, which seemed to be a minor artery of traffic. There was a similar public-house at this corner as well, which looked as though it was the only flourishing thing in its immediate neighbourhood. There seemed to be nothing in the district to enliven the period of waiting.

After a short stroll of exploration, Harold discovered that parallel with Inkerman Street ran an almost identical thoroughfare, which he identified as Balaclava Street. The houses bearing even numbers in Inkerman Street stood back to back with those bearing odd numbers in Balaclava Street, with only narrow back-yards, divided by a low wall, between them. But, walking down Balaclava Street, Harold noticed that there was an exception to this rule. Between numbers 35 and 37 was the opening of a narrow passage, not more than four feet wide, running between the high walls of the houses on either side. Harold stopped and looked down it, wondering vaguely if it led through to Inkerman Street, and if so, why he had not noticed its opposite end. He found, however, that it was apparently a cul-de-sac, terminated by doors on either side, which presumably opened into the back-yards of two of the houses, but whether these fronted Inkerman or Balaclava Street he could not determine.

It was rapidly growing dark, and a fine rain was beginning to fall. A lamplighter was coming along Balaclava Street, kindling the yellow gas-flames as he came along. He stopped opposite Harold, pushed a long stick into the lamp beside him, and went on his way. Harold shivered suddenly. This was a beastly neighbourhood, the sort of place where one might expect anything to happen. The gloomy passage appeared all at once dark and furtive, as though it might harbour any kind of evil shadows. The light of the lamp scarcely penetrated it more than a few feet; beyond that it stretched dark and sinister. Harold glanced at it once more, then, almost with a feeling of relief, moved on. It was nearly five o'clock.

He had not proceeded many steps before a man, walking rapidly and muffled up in a heavy overcoat and scarf, hurried past him. Harold, with plenty of time on his hands to kill, had sufficient curiosity to glance over his shoulder to have another look at him. There was something about the man, his clothes, his walk, that seemed ill-fitted to the squalor of Balaclava Street. It was as though he were not flesh and blood, but the ghost of one of those respectable clerks of long ago, come back to revisit the scene of his former life. And then, just as Harold turned to continue his way, the man dived suddenly into the dark passage.

The illusion of his spiritual origin seemed complete for the moment, and Harold smiled at the illustration of his thought. That passage looked haunted, it was quite natural that a ghost should choose it as his terrestrial habitat. As a matter of fact, the man must be some poor devil who owned a room at the back of one of these decayed houses, and preferred to let himself in at the back door rather than traverse a filthy hall such as had been revealed by many of the open doors he had passed. No doubt the district held many such tragedies. Harold felt the place getting on his nerves. In ten minutes or so, the time it would take him to stroll out of Balaclava Street round into Inkerman Street, he would knock once more on the door of Number 36. If the 'nevvy' were there, so much the better. If not, he would chuck the business up and go home.

As it happened, he was lucky. The door of Mr Samuels' shop was open when he reached it. He mounted the steps, paused a moment on the threshold, then grasped the handle. The door opened inwards with a prodigious creaking of hinges, and Harold was immediately aware of a strange coughing and wheezing somewhere in the interior of the house. Evidently Mr Samuels' complaint was some form of asthma or bronchitis. Harold found himself hoping that it was sufficiently serious to keep him in bed during his visit.

The front door opened into a narrow hall, off which was a second door leading into what he recognised as the front shop. Just enough space had been cleared among the rubbish that lumbered it to allow of a passage from the door to a dirty counter, almost hidden beneath the miscellaneous articles which covered it, and another passage from the back of the counter to a second door. Judging by the sounds which came through this, Harold guessed that it led to a back room in which the invalid was living. Mr Samuels appeared to be engaged in an altercation with someone, no doubt his nephew. Harold could hear muttered words between the fits of coughing, and occasionally a sharp, almost falsetto voice, apparently raised in self-excuse. He rapped on the counter and waited.

The shop was very dark. A gleam of light came through the slightly-opened door leading into the back room; the last fading rays of daylight, aided by the reflection of a street lamp outside, fell upon the dirty furniture just inside the uncurtained window. It was evident that artificial light was not one of Mr Samuels' extravagances, and it suddenly struck Harold that perhaps this economy was in part practised out of consideration for his visitors. From what he had learnt from Mr Boost, it seemed quite probable that the antique business was nothing but a blind to cover more sinister dealings. Harold began to wonder whether he had not set his feet on perilous ground, in thus undertaking to be an intermediary between Mr Boost and Mr Samuels, alias Szamuelly.

The argument in the back room continued meanwhile, and Harold rapped on the counter a second time, more loudly. There was a hoarse growl from the back, a fit of coughing, then silence. Suddenly the door opened. Harold caught a glimpse of an untidy room, and the door shut again behind the form of a young man, whose face was indistinguishable in the prevailing darkness.

The young man advanced warily to the back of the counter, and peered at his visitor. 'What d'yer want?' he enquired in the curious falsetto voice Harold had already overheard.

'I came to make an enquiry on Mr Boost's behalf,' began Harold. 'He asked me to come and see Mr Samuels—'

The young man leaned over the counter confidentially, and Harold saw that he had long black hair falling down on either side of his face, like the typical Galician Jew.

''E's in bed,' he whispered. 'Ha, ha, ha! In bed, an' that bad-tempered I 'ardly dare go near 'im. 'Ush, 'e's listening!'

The young man drew back, and stood bolt upright for a minute, as though expecting a minatory voice from the back room. But the silence remained unbroken, and the young man turned to Harold once more.

'You daren't say much when 'e's about,' he explained. 'Wot is it you want to know?'

'I understand that some days ago, last Monday week to be exact, Mr Samuels sent a bale of goods to Mr Boost,' replied Harold. 'He asked me to find out what was in it.'

'Oh, my! ain't 'e got it then?' exclaimed the young man in alarm. 'Uncle'll raise 'ell if he 'ears of that. Packed 'em up myself and gave 'em to the carter, I did. "See you takes that to Mr Boost's shop at once," I says. "If 'e ain't there, shove 'em under the porch, they'll be all right." Oh, lor, if 'e ain't got 'em!'

'I expect he'll get them all right,' replied Harold, mindful of Mr Boost's injunction not to let Samuels know of the disappearance of the bale. 'You see, he's away, and he asked me to find out what the stuff was, as he hadn't heard from Mr Samuels.'

'You workin' for old Boost, then?' whispered the young man.

Harold nodded. After all, in a sense, he was.

'That's all right then,' replied the young man. 'I'll tell you. It was some stuff Uncle thought 'e could do with. One o' them grandfather clock-cases, no works with it, and 'alf a dozen brass statuettes. 'Eavy they was, too. The statuettes was put inside the case, and the lot wrapped up in matting. That'll be the bale 'e means?'

'That's it,' said Harold. This fitted the description given by George. 'Thanks very much, I'll tell Mr Boost.'

He turned to leave the shop, then hesitated. 'I don't think you need mention it to Mr Samuels,' he said.

The young man giggled. 'I won't tell 'im, never fear,' he replied.

As Harold left the shop he once more heard the menacing voice from the back room, apparently raised in anger.

CHAPTER VI

As Harold made his way back to Riverside Gardens he fully determined never again to run errands for Mr Boost to his friends. The Samuels' menage, the formidable and asthmatic old man, whose voice was quite sufficient to confirm Mr Boost's unfavourable description, and his apparently half-witted nephew, were quite enough to deter him from any further experiments in that direction.

Mr Boost, to whom he disclosed this intention with considerable emphasis, received it with much amusement. 'Inkerman Street too rough for you, was it?' he said. 'You want to wait till the Dictatorship of the Proletariat comes along, young man. Then you'll be glad enough to pick up crusts in a tidy sight worse place than that. We'll give you blinkin' bourgeois a taste of what the workers have to suffer now, that we will. You wait an' see!'

Mr Boost paused for a moment, rapt in contemplation of that millennium of which he never ceased to dream.

'However, perhaps you could learn to be useful in time,' he continued in a more kindly tone, as of one who sees a faint hope of promise in an otherwise desperate character. 'Lucky for you you saw young Isidore, and not the old man. He'd have sent you about your business sharp enough. Grandfather clock-case, was it? That's true enough, I expect. Old Samuels knows I plants new works in 'em and sells 'em all about the country for capitalists to buy at big prices. And the statuettes? Like enough. Wonderful what a bit o' faking will do for them, too.'

'But who on earth would steal stuff like that?' enquired Harold, interested far more in the bale itself than in its contents.

Mr Boost shrugged his shoulders. 'Somebody who wanted to do me a bad turn, I suppose,' he replied. 'This world ain't full o' dear friends, not by a long chalk. Lots o' people know I have valuable stuff lying about sometimes. Nice suck-in they must have had when they opened that lot, though.' And Mr Boost chuckled with some approach to pleasantry.

Harold left him, still convinced that there must be some connection between the disappearance of the grandfather clock and the dead man in his bedroom. Two such unusual occurrences would hardly have taken place on the same evening entirely independently of one another. He spent the remainder of the evening racking his brains for some possible connection between the two, and finally decided to tell the whole story to Professor Priestley.

In pursuance of this idea, he arrived at Westbourne Terrace about three o'clock the following afternoon, and found the eminent mathematician in his study. He was greeted with considerable affability, tempered with a suggestion of stern scrutiny of which he could scarcely fail to be conscious. It was without surprise that he heard the Professor's first question.

'Well, my boy, and what have you been doing since I saw you last?'

'I've been trying to get to the bottom of this business, sir,' replied Harold. 'I haven't seen any of the set I used to spend my time with since it happened.'

The Professor nodded his head appreciatively. 'I am delighted to hear it,' he said. 'May I assume that you adhere to your intention to lead a more useful life in future?'

'You may, sir,' replied Harold fervently. 'If only I could get clear of this beastly suspicion—'

'You must not let that weigh too heavily upon you,' interrupted the Professor. 'You have friends, myself among them, who are convinced that you are in no way implicated in the events of that unfortunate night. I have been considering the matter, and have reached certain conclusions, deduced logically, from the facts I have ascertained. I do not propose to repeat these conclusions at the present stage, lest they should prejudice you in favour of any particular theory. Now, have you discovered any additional data of which you consider I should be informed?'

'Well, I don't know, sir,' replied Harold doubtfully. 'It may or may not be a coincidence, but there was rather a curious robbery at Number 16 that very night.'

'A robbery!' repeated the Professor sharply. 'What of? Let me have the particulars as you know them.'

Harold gave an account of his interview with Mr Boost, and of that comrade's annoyance at the disappearance of his bale of goods. When he had finished, the Professor sat for a few minutes in silence, and then began to speak, more, as it seemed, to an imaginary audience of students than to Harold.

'Here we have a case of an alleged disappearance which requires careful examination before it can be admitted within the domain of fact. We have first to establish the existence of the matter alleged to have disappeared, in this case a bale of goods, stated to be of a certain size, shape and weight. You will observe that the intended recipient of this bale has, according to his own account, never seen it, nor was it discovered by the police on the morning after the crime. The only direct evidence of its existence so far is that of one George, a carter, who may never have delivered it. This evidence, again, is only reported by the intended recipient, who may have invented the whole story for some purpose of his own.

'Presuming, however, that this bale did exist, and was actually delivered and placed in the porch of Number 16 some time during that particular evening, we are led to enquire into its subsequent history. A bale of that size and shape would be difficult to move far without means of transport, the provision of which would pre-suppose a definite plot for its removal. On the other hand, a strong man could have rolled it across the front garden, lifted it over the wall, and pitched it into the canal. A third possibility is that the bale, as such, was never removed at all, but unpacked on the spot and its contents removed piecemeal. You follow me?'

'Exactly, sir,' replied Harold. 'I confess that I had never examined these alternatives, though. From the contents of the bale, I should think that your last possibility was the most likely one.'

'Ah, you ascertained the contents?' enquired the Professor. 'Excellent. Tell me as exactly as you can how you did so.'

'I went to see this man Samuels, who despatched the bale to Mr Boost,' replied Harold, with a pardonable air of self-satisfaction.

'Ah, that is very interesting,' commented the Professor. 'Give me an account, as minute as possible, of your interview.'

'Well, I didn't exactly see him, sir,' replied Harold. 'I heard him, though, and I had a talk with his nephew, who told me that he had packed the bale himself, and delivered it to George the carter, which confirms George's own statement to Mr Boost. This nephew, whose name is Isidore Samuels, told me that the bale contained the case of a grandfather-clock and some bronze statuettes. Mr Boost agrees that it is most likely that Mr Samuels should have sent him such a consignment, and that a bale containing such things would be of the size and shape that George described.'

Again the Professor remained plunged in thought for some little time before replying. 'Unless, then, we assume collusion between this Isidore Samuels and George the carter, an assumption which the theory of probability forbids me to make under the circumstances, the existence of the bale is provisionally established,' he said at last. 'I say provisionally, for we have no confirmation of the statements of either Boost or Isidore Samuels. We do not even know that such a man as George the carter really exists. This is a point that you might ascertain for yourself. But, before we go any further, I should like a full account of your visit to Samuels' place of business. Tell me your procedure, omitting no detail, however apparently irrelevant.'

Harold complied with the greatest readiness. He had half expected the Professor to brush aside the incident of the bale of goods as having no bearing whatever on his own case. He began by recounting how Mr Boost had described the locality of Samuels' shop and the characteristics of its occupant. The Professor listened intently, and stopped him as soon as he began to give an account of his journey.

'Here is a map of London,' he said. 'Come to my desk and trace your route as accurately as you can with this pencil. Yes, that is where you dismounted from the tram. Inkerman Street must lie in this direction. Ah, here it is. But this map is on too small a scale to assist us much further.'

He opened a drawer and produced a pad of paper. 'Here is some squared paper,' he continued. 'Draw me a rough plan, as nearly to scale as you can, explaining your movements after you reached the corner of Inkerman Street.'

Harold continued his narration, indicating with the pencil the position of Number 36, the doorway where he stood talking with the man in shirt-sleeves, his subsequent wanderings into Balaclava Street, even the narrow entry which had thrilled him with superstitious horror. The Professor took up his rough plan and looked at it with interest.

'According to this, the narrow passage in Balaclava Street very nearly corresponds with the back of Samuels' shop in Inkerman Street,' commented the Professor. 'Is this accidental, or did you notice it at the time?'

'No, 'pon my soul, I didn't, sir,' replied Harold in surprise. 'Now I come to think of it, though, it does exactly. By Jove, that's a queer thing, now you mention it. I saw a fellow enter the passage just as I left it. I noticed him particularly, he was a respectable-looking sort of chap, gave me the impression that he was ashamed of being seen in that sort of neighbourhood.'

The Professor nodded. 'Very well,' he said. 'Continue your account.'

Harold described his return to Inkerman Street, his entrance into the shop, its appearance, the altercation he overheard between Samuels and his nephew. The Professor interrupted him from time to time, requesting additional information upon the smallest details. 'Have you any reason to connect the man you saw enter the passage with this Isidore Samuels?' he asked finally. 'If your sketch is correct, it is possible that the shop has a back door opening into this passage, and Isidore might use this entrance upon his return.'

'Oh, dear no, sir,' replied Harold with a smile. 'They were different types altogether. Of course, I didn't see their faces, it was much too dark for that. Isidore was—well, what you might expect the nephew of a man with a name like Szamuelly, who keeps a junk shop in Camberwell, to be. The other chap attracted my attention just because he wasn't that sort at all. He gave me a kind of impression that he was—well, the sort of fellow one meets in one's own circle.'

'Ah! Well, tell me what happened when Isidore left the back room and came into the shop.'

Harold finished the account of the evening's proceedings without further interruption. The Professor listened carefully, and when he had finished, glanced up at the clock.

'I see it is nearly half past four,' he remarked. 'Shall we go into the drawing-room, and see whether April has some tea for us?'

Harold flushed crimson. 'I—er—' he stammered. 'I don't think that April—'

'Nonsense, nonsense!' interrupted the Professor. 'April will be very glad to see you. She shares my views as to your innocence in this matter. I have intimated to her that you have—er—abandoned your former methods of living, and she shares my approbation. Come along, my boy.'

The Professor led the way to the first floor, and opened the door of a room that Harold remembered so well. April was alone, and jumped up from her chair as they entered.

She was a strikingly pretty girl, tall and graceful, with fair hair and a pair of blue eyes that seemed full of the delight of life. As she came across the room to him Harold realised for the first time what an utter ass he had been to play the fool and waste his chances so far as she was concerned. Where could he find anything that could compensate him for the loss of her?

But she gave him no time for any such dismal reflections. 'Hullo, Harold, old dear,' she exclaimed. 'I am glad Father brought you up. Mary told me you were here, so I told her not to let anyone else in. Come and sit on the sofa here and tell me all about yourself.'

Harold surrendered without further ado, and the Professor, displaying an unsuspected tact, discovered that he had left his glasses downstairs.

April, with a sudden access of seriousness, took Harold's hands in hers, and looked him straight in the face.

'You've been a bit of a rotter,' she said. 'Chuck it up, and let's be pals again like we used to be. I know as well as Father that you hadn't anything to do with the old blighter who died in your rooms. It was just a bit of rotten luck, and that's the end of it. Now, come and see me again as you used to. Swear?'

The familiar word, which they had always used as children to seal their mutual compacts, brought rather a wry smile to Harold's lips.

'Swear!' he repeated obediently. 'But, April, it can't be like it was then. I've been much more of a rotter than you know—'

'I wonder!' interrupted April gaily. 'I know better than most people what you're capable of. Here's Father back again, and tea.'

During the meal Harold was vividly conscious that both Professor Priestley and April were doing their best to make him feel that the years of his backsliding had been forgotten, and that he was once more to be accepted as the oldest friend of the family. He, who had looked upon himself as an outcast, felt that here at least was sympathy and understanding. In his gratitude he resolved that he would leave no stone unturned to clear himself, to justify himself in the eyes of those who trusted him. But—no further advance was possible. The past, with its dark shadows, could not be disposed of so easily. Vere—Vere waited somewhere in the background, Vere with her intangible claims upon him, waiting to drag him back from this peaceful room—

The clock struck five, and as it did so the door opened, and Mary appeared. 'Mr Denbigh,' she announced.

A young man, carefully dressed, clean-shaven and good looking, with the air of a student relieved somewhat by a humorous twinkle in his eyes, entered and shook hands with the Professor.

'Hullo, Evan!' exclaimed April. 'What are you doing here? I thought you were working every evening with Sir Alured?'

'When the cat's away, the mice will play,' replied Denbigh. 'My revered chief is reading a paper before some learned society this evening, so I just ran over to tell you that I had a couple of tickets for a show on Saturday. I can't stop long.'

He turned to Harold and held out his hand. 'I'm awfully glad to see you again, Merefield,' he said warmly, and then, in a lower tone, 'I've been waiting for a chance to tell you how sorry I am about all this business. You know perfectly well that I don't believe a word of all the rot that's been said about you.'

Harold muttered some incoherent words of thanks, but the Professor interrupted him.

'Sit down, Denbigh,' he said. 'You can give us a few minutes, at least. Faversham is not such a hard taskmaster as to begrudge you that leisure. Harold and I have been discussing that extraordinary affair at his rooms the other night, and we should be glad to hear your views upon it.'

Denbigh laughed, almost apologetically. 'If you'll allow me to say so, sir, I hardly think it's worth much consideration,' he replied. 'Of course, I can imagine how Harold feels about it, and I'm awfully sorry for him. But, after all, the thing's practically blown over already. We don't know who the fellow was, I admit, but it was merely a case of death from natural causes, duly certified—'

'Natural causes!' interrupted the Professor testily. 'It may seem to be natural causes from the point of view of you medical men, but to the student of the exact sciences it is nothing of the kind. For an individual to deposit his dead body upon the bed of a complete stranger is anything but natural. It is, in fact, a most indecent and unusual proceeding.'

The Professor paused a moment, as though challenging his hearers to deny his statement. As nobody ventured to do so, he proceeded.

'We have here a somewhat unusual instance of irregularity. In most similar cases we are faced with a disappearance, or, at least, with a corpse which can be identified. Here we have a corpse which, so far, has not been identified, and no corresponding disappearance. We can, therefore, form no theory to account, not for the cause of the unknown individual's death, but for his dead body being found on Harold's bed. Until we can form such a theory, and test it by facts, I do not at present see how we shall arrive at the solution.'

'As a theoretical problem, I admit its interest, sir,' ventured Denbigh. 'But I still believe that, as a practical event, we shall hear no more about it.'

He rose from his chair as he spoke. 'I must dash back now,' he continued. 'Really, Mr Denbigh, I am surprised that you should absent yourself at a time when we have so much research upon our hands! I have observed that the young man of today is far too much inclined to place the gratification of his pleasures before the requirements of his career—'

He mimicked the voice and mannerisms of Sir Alured Faversham so perfectly that even the Professor smiled.

'Add that the young man of today seems to be lacking in respect for his seniors,' he said. 'Well, we will not detain you. Remember me to Faversham when you see him.'

Denbigh took his departure, and after a short interval Harold, having promised to return within a few days, or even earlier if he had anything to report, left the house in his turn. His road to Riverside Gardens was darkened by the contemplation of what he had so wilfully thrown away.

CHAPTER VII

IT was dark before Harold reached Riverside Gardens, so dark that he did not notice the figure waiting by the entrance of the cul-de-sac until she was only a few paces distant. And by then, of course, it was too late to avoid her.

She ran up to him and laid a hand upon his arm. 'Harold!' she exclaimed in a low, not unmusical voice. 'I thought you were never coming back! Where have you been?'

He paused a moment, confused and irresolute. The influence of April was strong upon him, the determination to cast aside the old past life and qualify afresh for a more reputable existence was still of too tender a growth to be exposed to temptation. She saw his hesitation and pressed closer to him.

'You're not cross?' she pleaded. 'I know I haven't been near you for a long time, but—oh, I can't explain, it's a long story. And I've been waiting here for ever so long.'

Harold's mind was made up. He could not avoid the meeting, could not say what he must to her out here in the open street. Automatically his arm slipped into hers. 'Come along, Vere, old thing,' he said, and the girl gladly fell into step with him.

Neither spoke a word until they reached Harold's rooms, and there she flung herself into a chair as he busied himself lighting the lamp. As the flame grew you would have seen that she was dark, not perhaps pretty, but with a pair of eyes that somehow intrigued you, led you on to look at them again in the endeavour to fathom their attraction. And in them was an invitation, an appeal to the sensual side of your nature, which to your experience might have hinted danger. Add to this that she was plainly, almost severely dressed, and you have the impression that Vera Donaldson, known to her intimates as Vere, conveyed to the world at large.

'I came straight round from the office,' she said, as Harold sat himself on the arm of her chair, to which she had beckoned him. 'I simply had to come, dear, if only to tell you how sorry I am about all this wretched business. I thought you'd write to me, but as you didn't, I simply couldn't wait any longer.'

'I thought you'd forgotten me,' replied Harold slowly, seeking the opening which would enable him to tell her that their intimacy must cease. 'I waited for you that night at the Naxos, and you didn't turn up—'

'I know, Harold dear,' she interrupted. 'And that's one of the things I had to say to you.' She paused, and for a long minute there was silence in the room, broken only by the distant rumbling of the traffic over the canal bridge.

'I've told you before that—that there's been another man in my life besides you,' she began again abruptly.

Harold nodded. From the very first she had hinted that she was not entirely a free agent, that somewhere in the background stood a figure which in some way cast a shadow over her life. Not that there had ever been any question of marriage between them; each had avoided the suggestion as though by tacit understanding.

'He knew I used to come here,' she continued, and then, seeing the look of concern on Harold's face, she laughed, almost merrily.

'Oh, that didn't matter. It was no business of his, anyhow. I didn't tell him, but—well, I may as well tell you. He used to come and see me sometimes, to—to get a few shillings out of me. I cared for him once, you know, and I used to give him money when I had any to spare. One day he must have followed me out—I was dressing to go out with you, and I wouldn't see him—and saw me go into the Naxos Club. I suppose he waited outside, for when I next saw him he told me he had seen me leave there and get into a taxi with you. He managed to find out who you were and where you lived.'

'How the devil did he do that?' exclaimed Harold in astonishment.

Vere shrugged her shoulders. 'Oh, I don't know,' she replied carelessly. 'He's as cunning as a bagful of monkeys, and it wouldn't be very difficult. One of the waiters at the Naxos, perhaps; they know all about the members. Anyhow, he came to me about a fortnight ago, looking jolly smart. I thought he wanted more money, but he said he didn't, that he knew how to make a lot more money than I could ever give him. Then he made me the offer.'

'What offer?' asked Harold, seeing her pause in embarrassment.

'Why, that he—wouldn't worry me any more, would leave the coast clear for me, as he put it. Said as I'd found someone else, I'd better get on with it and make the best of it.'

'Devilish considerate of him, I must say,' said Harold sarcastically.

'Yes, but there were conditions,' replied Vere. 'I was to make an appointment to meet you at the Naxos on a certain night, and then not to go. After that I was not to see you for ten days, when I was to be free to see as much as I pleased of you, and good luck to me. I wouldn't consent to this at first, but he threatened to make an awful fuss if I didn't. He knew I worked at the Women's Social League, and he swore he'd turn up there and make a scene. He knew as well as I did that I'd lose my job if they knew anything about him, or you, or the Naxos, so at last I agreed. And then, when I saw the papers the day after I was to have met you, I nearly went mad. I wanted to come and help you somehow, but I had sworn not to see you. I tried to get hold of him and tell him our bargain was off, but I couldn't find him. And then I thought—'

But Harold had leapt from the arm of his chair and stood confronting her.

'The night you were to have met me!' he exclaimed. 'But—that was the very night—'

'Yes, I know,' replied Vere remorsefully. 'Now you see the fright I had. I thought there must be some connection. Then I went to see the body of the man you found here—the police let me in when I made up some story of a missing uncle—and I found a perfect stranger. It can't have been anything to do with him, after all.'

'Nonsense!' said Harold angrily. 'It can't be a coincidence that this fellow, whoever he is, got you to keep me out of the way on the very night I found a man dead in my bed. Look here, Vere, I've never asked you any questions, you know, but I'm going to ask them now. You've got to tell me who this fellow is. I want a word with him badly.'

Vere put out a hand and laid it on his arm. 'Don't be silly, dear,' she said. 'What's the good of making a fuss now? The whole thing's blown over; the man, whoever he was, died a natural death; it isn't as if there was any suggestion of you having murdered him. Besides, don't you see that I'm only free if I keep my—my friend's name dark? He'd take jolly good care to queer my pitch with you if I let you loose at him.'

The tone of Vere's voice, the thinly-veiled implication that she expected him to take advantage of this new freedom of hers, drove Harold to exasperation.

'I'm afraid I can't help that,' he replied. 'This business has sickened me of all that sort of thing. All I care about now is to clear up this infernal mystery. And as soon as I've done that I mean to run straight in future.'

Vere laughed, harshly and mockingly 'Run straight!' she echoed. 'Merry Devil run straight! That'll make some of them laugh, won't it?'

She flung herself back in her chair, and looked at him tantalisingly. 'After all,' she continued, 'I can't see that there's anything to prevent you indulging your new hobby. You might even marry me, you know.'

'Marry you!' he retorted hotly. 'Not likely. I don't propose to continue our acquaintance in future. Tell me the name of the fellow who took such a confounded interest in my movements that night, and we'll say good-bye.'

Vere's eyes flashed dark with anger, but she made no movement, only laughed, more softly this time.

'Oh-h!' she said slowly. 'So that's the game, is it? Get what you want from me, and then chuck me over like a sack of potatoes! My good innocent friend, do you really suppose that I shall fall in with your little plans as quietly as that?'

'I don't see what the devil you can do,' replied Harold. 'If you've any claims upon me, I'll pay them in cash somehow. I'll pay you for the name of your lover too, if that's what you want.'

Vere leaped from her chair and faced him, at last inflamed to fury. 'Thank you,' she hissed. 'Now I know exactly what to do. I fancy you'll regret this evening's work for the rest of your life, my friend.'

She turned from him, and made towards the door, but Harold sprang across the room and put his back to it. 'No you don't,' he exclaimed. 'Not until you tell me that fellow's name.'

Vere leant forward, glaring at him with a tigerish ferocity that revealed the true degradation of her nature. Harold had never seen her like this; she seemed the incarnation of evil, revolting, terrifying him. In spite of himself he shrank from her, as though fearing that she would touch him, and by that touch contaminate him irrevocably.

'Let me go!' she stormed. 'Open that door at once, or I'll shout until there's a crowd round the house. And a fine story I'll have for them, too, let me tell you. You'd enjoy a scene like that, coming on top of the one you've been through. A charge of that kind would help you to run straight, as you call it, wouldn't it? Let me go, you damned fool! Help!'

Her cry, shrill and piercing, rang through Harold's brain till it seemed to him as though the whole city must hear it. In one vivid instant he pictured April, Professor Priestley, Evan Denbigh, all the friends he had left, shunning him at the stroke of this new disgrace. Beaten, outwitted, he flung the door open.

Vere passed him without a word, without a glance. For many seconds he stood irresolute, listening to her footsteps as they passed down the stairs, through the front door, and died away along Riverside Gardens. Then he slammed the door and sank once more into his chair, his head hidden in his hands, despairing.

It was some long time before he could bring himself to think coherently and then at last he realised to the full what a fool he had been. He had lost his temper, had demeaned himself to Vere's own level in a battle of abuse, in which he had got distinctly the worst of it. The maddening thought that Vere held what was almost certainly the clue to the mystery tortured him. The clue had been within his grasp, and by his own senseless folly he had allowed it to escape him!

His first impulse was to leap up and follow Vere to her rooms, to persuade her somehow to disclose the identity of this mysterious friend or lover of hers. But a moment's reflection convinced him that this would be worse than useless. In Vere's present mood the only thing that could appease her would be complete surrender, and that involved more than he cared to contemplate. He had been fond of her once, had even, at times, wondered whether love had not coloured his passion. Now he knew that it was passion alone that had attracted him, that anything further between them was impossible, horrible to contemplate. If she were indeed free, free from what sordid bond he neither knew nor cared, he was bound—by the intangible bonds of an unattainable dream, if you will—to a far higher ideal. No, he must leave Vere to go her own way, with her sinister knowledge, her parting threats. There could be no hope of salvation through her.

Thus Harold, in the mood of exaltation which followed his outburst of temper. The image of April still haunted him, although he felt the hopelessness of any endeavour to return to the intimacy he had so wilfully cast away. Apart from anything else, there was Evan Denbigh, just the sort of fellow who would naturally appeal to her; clever, promising, with a fund of talent denied to himself. Oh, yes, they were admirably suited to one another. Take one small detail, for instance. April was an ardent lover of the stage, a love which found expression in her frequent appearance in amateur theatricals. Her face, her voice, her figure, all suited her appearance in any role she cared to study. Denbigh, he knew, was equally keen, a really capable actor, who had won warm commendation from competent critics. There were a thousand things these two had in common. Harold searched his brain for a single instance where he could shine in April's eyes. His writing? She had admitted that *Aspasia* had amused her. But—well, *Aspasia* was Vere, not April.

His reverie was interrupted by a heavy footfall on the stairs, and by a thundering knock in which he recognised the hard knuckles of his landlord. He opened the door, and Mr Boost entered unceremoniously.

'I haven't heard no more about that bale of mine,' he began abruptly. 'I'm beginning to think there's some hanky-panky about the whole business. More in it than what the eye sees, I mean.'

Harold made no reply, and Mr Boost puffed at his pipe, surrounding himself with an area of smoke through which his eyes gleamed darkly.

'Old Szamuelly 'll be getting more'n he likes one o' these days,' he continued. 'It's my belief this illness o' his is all my eye. He don't care to go outside his own place, I reckon.'

'Why, what has he done?' enquired Harold encouragingly.

'Done? Why I don't suppose he's done anything. He hasn't the pluck,' replied Mr Boost. 'But some o' the comrades' secrets has been getting about lately. The blasted bourgeois and their police have got hold of a thing or two that's made things awkward for some. Somebody's been giving the game away, and I shouldn't be surprised to find it was that old swine. I've a good mind to go and have a word with him, sick or not sick.'

'And tell him you've lost that bale?' suggested Harold maliciously.

'Bale be blowed!' replied Mr Boost. 'I've got to be away over the week-end. But on Monday evening I'll run over to Camberwell and have a little talk to Samuels and that blasted nephew of his. I'll learn 'em a lesson, you mark my words.'

A sudden idea struck Harold. The disappearance of the bale haunted him, and here might be an opportunity of hearing more about it.

'I'll come too, if I may,' he said quietly.

Mr Boost regarded him in astonishment. 'Well, I don't see why you shouldn't,' he said slowly. 'I'd like to know whether you told the truth about that other evening. But you'll have to stop outside while I have my little talk.'

'Oh, I wouldn't intrude for the world,' replied Harold lightly. 'I'll keep Isidore in play while you have it out with the old man, if you like.'

Mr Boost grunted, knocked his pipe out into the fireplace, and left the room abruptly. Harold was once more left to his own thoughts and his own longings.

CHAPTER VIII

SATURDAY passed uneventfully. Much as Harold longed for the atmosphere of Westbourne Terrace, he felt that he dared not go there without some reasonable excuse to see the Professor. Besides, it was the week-end, when Evan Denbigh might reasonably be expected to be free from his labours. And, hopeless though he knew his own cause to be, he felt no desire to see April and Denbigh together.

He had for a moment wondered whether he should tell the Professor about Vere and the strange clue she held. But his mind revolted from the idea. Any mention of Vere must necessarily lead to a confession he shrank from making, a confession which could only lower him in the Professor's eyes without bringing any corresponding advantage. If this clue were to be traced, it was he himself who must do it. He, alone and unaided, must find this man who had an interest in his absence from his rooms on the fatal night. He spent the day wandering disconsolately about London, seeing in every glance an accusation, in every passer-by a potential unbeliever in his innocence.

Mrs Clapton rested from her labours on Sundays, and as a rule Harold was undisturbed until such time as he chose to boil a kettle for himself. On this particular Sunday morning he slept late after a nightmare-ridden night. But his sleep was rudely broken by a persistent knocking. He rose wearily and opened the door to admit Mr Boost, stern-faced, and bearing in his hand the ample pages of *The Weekly Record*.

'Look here,' he said gruffly. 'I'd like to know what this means, if you don't mind.'

Harold took the paper from him and looked at it dully. *The Weekly Record* owed its enormous circulation to its graphic and sensational reports of crime, violence and frailty, duly introduced with appropriate headlines. The page Mr Boost held open for his inspection was headed 'The Mysterious Disappearance of Mr Sharp,' and beneath was a heavily leaded paragraph: '*The Weekly Record* is fortunate in having secured the services of a well-known writer, who prefers to hide his identity under the pseudonym of "W." This gentleman is a keen student of crime, and in the following story he suggests a solution to a type of unsolved mystery such as has frequently puzzled the authorities. Readers of *The Weekly Record* will understand that, though W.'s deductions are dressed in the garb of pure fiction, they are nevertheless the result of earnest study of actual facts. It is scarcely necessary to add that all names and places mentioned are purely fictitious.'

Harold read this without interest. 'What the devil has all this got to do with me?' he asked impatiently. 'I can't say I am particularly interested in sensational crime stories.'

'Aren't you?' replied Mr Boost. 'I'm not so sure. You read this one and see.'

Something in Mr Boost's manner sent an uncomfortable thrill down Harold's back and he turned to the paper once more with a foreboding interest.

W's story, though told as fiction, was, in fact, a reconstruction of the 'Paddington Mystery', as it had come to be known, as imagined by the writer. The principal figure in the story was a young man of dissolute habits, who had constructed a liaison with the daughter of a clerk engaged in a garage. The girl, abandoned by this heartless seducer, took to the streets as a means of earning her livelihood, but not before an unguarded word had revealed to her broken-hearted parent the name and address of the man who had betrayed her. The father, rendered desperate by his failure to obtain an interview with the latter, determined to secure access to his rooms during his absence and confront him upon his return. To do this it was necessary to swim a river and break open a window. He accomplished the feat successfully, but his efforts proved too much for a delicate constitution, and he collapsed on his enemy's bed.

The hero of the story was a young man, equipped with the mental apparatus of the usual detective of fiction. Starting from the assumption that although no actual crime had been committed, a great injustice had been done, he sought for the cause of the unknown man's entry to the villain's rooms, and by a series of coincidences, came into contact with the girl, who was in ignorance of her father's death. The story ended with a scene in which the girl and her seducer were brought together. The latter was overcome by remorse before the irrefutable logic of the amateur detective, and made an offer of honourable marriage which was gratefully accepted.

The whole thing was admirably calculated to appeal to the sentiment of the readers of *The Weekly Record*, but there was far more in it than that. The events to which it referred were as perfectly obvious as they were doubtless intended to be, and few people reading the story could have resisted the impression that it was a remarkably plausible theory to account for the Paddington mystery. That Mr Boost regarded it as such was palpable.

He waited until Harold had read it through, then, as their eyes met, laughed harshly.

'You're a nice young fellow, aren't you?' he said. 'I've seen that girl come in here with my own eyes, I have. Pretty scrape you've got yourself into with a bit of skirt, too. What are you going to do about it?'

'What the devil do you mean?' replied Harold angrily. 'You don't suppose there's a word of truth in all this trash, do you? I tell you I didn't know the man who was found dead in here from Adam.'

Mr Boost puffed at his pipe, wholly unconvinced. 'Where's that girl you used to bring in here?' he asked gruffly.

'I don't know, and I'm damned if I care,' replied Harold with considerable heat.

'Ah!' said Mr Boost, glancing significantly at the paper, which lay in a disordered heap on the floor. 'You don't know, eh? Perhaps she had a father, had she?'

The question of Vere's parentage had never occurred to Harold. 'Father?' he repeated. 'I'm blest if I know; I never asked her.'

'If that's so you wouldn't have known him from Adam if he had come and died on that there bed!' declared Mr Boost, triumphantly. 'Looks to me as if you'd have a job to prove that yarn weren't true.'

'It's all nonsense, I tell you,' began Harold angrily, but Mr Boost stopped him with uplifted hand.

'Well, you can't put up a better tale, anyhow,' he said. 'Oh, I don't give a cuss whether it's true or not, it's not my business, and one bourgeois more or less is neither here nor there. I shouldn't be sorry if it was true, for I don't mind telling you I've had my doubts that you know more about that missing bale of mine than you cared to say. Well, I'll leave you the paper; I thought that it might do you good to see it.'

He stumped out of the room, slamming the door behind him. Harold, confronted with this new development, sat for a while as if stunned. Who could have written this horrible libel (for such it was)? In whose interest could it be to drag the whole matter to light again, and to brand him with an infamous character in the process? The introduction of the girl into the case was an entirely new factor. Could the thing have been written by someone who knew of his intimacy with Vere? He racked his brains to think who, of his acquaintances of the Naxos Club, could have thought it worth while to make such a suggestion. It could have been nobody else; the existence of Vere he had always hidden carefully from the more respectable of his friends.

For a moment he wondered whether this solution of the mystery were correct, whether Vere really had a father, whether, if so, this man had come to remonstrate with him for his intimacy with her. But no, it could not be. Vere had seen the body, and had said herself that the man was an utter stranger to her, and this before they had quarrelled, and when she would have had nothing to gain by concealing the truth. No, the story was a fabrication, but it was none the less a fresh burden thrust upon him. He realised that April and the Professor must certainly see this loathsome calumny—*The Weekly Record*, though not circulating upstairs at Westbourne Terrace, was eagerly devoured by Mary in the seclusion of her pantry. And even if she refrained from telling the news, the circulation of the infernal rag was so extensive that some mutual acquaintance was bound to bring it to notice. In which case, how was he to clear himself without divulging the part Vere had played in his life?

Despairingly he picked up the paper once more, striving to find some glaring error in the story on which he could base his defiance. The infernal cleverness of the thing impressed itself upon him with greater force the more he read it. The process of deduction was merciless in its logic; it might have been the Professor himself who had penned it. The hero dealt with the man's disappearance almost in the Professor's own words. The very distinction which the Professor had drawn between 'natural causes' in the medical and the logical sense, was repeated and elaborated. The detective in the story had sought for a likely cause for a man of the deceased's type to force an entrance into the villain's rooms and had found it. So plausible was his theory, that it was practically certain to be believed, unless Harold himself produced witnesses to prove its falsity. And the only possible witness was Vere, whose mere appearance would damn him for ever in the eyes wherein he most sought justification. And Vere; Vere had given him a glimpse of the lengths to which she was prepared to go in the virulence of her fury. Almost her last words to him had been a threat; what, if she were to perjure herself and testify to the truth of the story?

He wrestled with the problem the whole morning and well on into the afternoon. Then suddenly he took the resolution with both hands, and, without giving time for his newly-found courage to cool, he left Riverside Gardens hastily and started for Westbourne Terrace. In the Professor lay his only hope; he would tell him the whole story and abide by his decision, whatever it might be. As he went, he wondered vaguely in what part of the Empire it would be best to bury a past which must exclude him for ever from the land of his birth.

The menacing calm of Sunday afternoon enfolded the virtuous thoroughfares of Bayswater, faintly redolent of the lingering odours of baked meats. A round-eyed housemaid, summoned by his ringing from some distant depths, opened the door to him. Mary was doubtless enjoying her day off in the bosom of some relative's family. Harold was conducted to the Professor's study, where he spent a bad five minutes alone, tempted by an overwhelming desire for sudden flight from those sacred precincts.

At last the Professor came in, briskly, as a man who would scorn to have it known that he sometimes indulged in a nap after lunch on Sunday.

'Well, my boy, I am very glad to see you,' he began affably. 'I am alone today, as it happens. Evan arrived this morning and carried April off to some entertainment which appeared to appeal to them both. Sit down, sit down. Have you anything to tell me?'

Harold's heart sank. It was evident from the warmth of this welcome that the Professor had not yet seen that fatal story in *The Weekly Record*. How should he begin the dreaded confession?

'Thank you, sir,' he began confusedly. Then abruptly he snatched the offending paper from his pocket and held it out, almost defiantly. 'There's a page in that rag I think you ought to read, sir,' he blurted out.

To his astonishment the Professor smiled, but made no effort to take the proffered paper.

'Excellent, my boy,' he said kindly. 'I am more than ever convinced of the genuineness of your repentance. I can guess what it cost you to bring me that newspaper. As a matter of fact, I have already read it with some considerable care. Evan brought a copy with him when he came this morning.'

'Then you don't believe it?' exclaimed Harold eagerly.

The Professor put the tips of his fingers together and gazed fixedly at the ceiling.

'The theory advanced in that narrative, thinly disguised as fiction, is extremely plausible,' he replied oracularly. 'There are, however, certain aspects of it which predispose me to doubt its correctness. It would assist me to hear your views upon it.'

Harold averted his eyes. 'The rotten thing about it is that there *was* a girl,' he mumbled. 'I ought to have told you about her before, sir, but until a couple of days ago I had no idea that she had anything to do with this business.'

The Professor paused a moment before replying. 'My dear boy, of course there was a girl,' he said at last kindly, in parental rather than professorial tones. 'I guessed that long ago, and the revelations consequent upon the disclosure of the Naxos Club were such as to strengthen my convictions. But at the same time, I am convinced that she had very little connection with the man found dead in your rooms. Unless, of course—how tall is she?'

Harold started at the abrupt question. 'Tall, sir?' he repeated. 'Why, I hardly know. Not much shorter than I am. Fairly tall for a girl—slim; it's difficult to describe her.'

'Of course it is,' replied the Professor. 'No two persons' accounts of the same human being ever agree; that is one of the first difficulties of a case like this. I shall have to see her for myself. Now, my boy, tell me in as few words as possible the history of your relations with her, especially shortly before and since the events we are investigating.'

In straightforward language Harold confessed the whole story of his intimacy with Vere, the meetings at the Naxos Club, her visits to him at Riverside Gardens. He explained how, on the fatal night, he had been expecting her at the Naxos Club and how he had seen nothing of her until that evening, two days ago, when she had waited for him at the end of Riverside Gardens. As exactly as he could, he repeated their conversation in his rooms, and concluded with the threats she had uttered on her departure. The Professor listened attentively, throwing in a question here and there, as was his wont. When Harold had finished he sat for a long time wrapt in thought.

'Of course, you were quite right to break off your relations with this young woman,' he said at length. 'It is, however, unfortunate that you should have quarrelled with her before she divulged the identity of the man who desired your absence from your rooms that night. I assume that you have no reason to doubt the truth of her story?'

'None at all, sir, though, of course, I have no means of confirming it,' replied Harold.

'Naturally,' agreed the Professor. Then suddenly, after a pause, 'Have you had the hasp of your window mended yet?' he enquired.

'Why, no, sir, I haven't,' replied Harold. 'You don't think that anyone else is likely to break in, do you?'

'Then leave it alone for the present,' said the Professor, ignoring his anxious enquiry. 'Now, my boy, I am not going to ask you to seek out Miss Vere Donaldson again. You have broken with her, and it is better that the cleavage should be permanent. If necessary, I will secure an interview with her myself. Meanwhile, do not worry about the plausible theory set out in *The Weekly Record*. I can assure you that it contains a flaw which is quite sufficient to destroy the whole argument.'

'What is that, sir?' enquired Harold eagerly.

The Professor immediately assumed his didactic tone. 'Until theories are submitted to the test of uncontrovertible facts, they are worthless,' he said. 'In due course I will present you with an explanation of the events of that night which will be proof against any attempts to destroy it. Until then, I must ask you to trust me.'

'Very well, sir,' said Harold. 'I know I can safely leave matters in your hands. Meanwhile, what can I do?'

'Stay where you are and wait,' replied the Professor kindly. 'I know that inaction is the hardest thing to demand, but, believe me, at this juncture it is necessary. By the way, when Miss Vere was in the habit of coming to your rooms, how did she gain access?'

'At first I used to let her in,' said Harold. 'Then, in case she should come when I was out, I gave her a key. She lost it very soon afterwards, though.'

'I see,' replied the Professor. Harold, guessing that the interview was at an end, and dreading the return of April and Evan, rose and took his leave.

The Professor sat for a long time after his departure, lost in thought. Then he took up the copy of *The Weekly Record* from the table on which Harold had left it, and read the story through once more with deep attention. 'I wonder!' he muttered as he flung it away in disgust. 'No, it is impossible! I must have facts, more facts!'

And with a face grave beyond his wont, he turned and left the room.

CHAPTER IX

On the following day, faithful to his promise, Mr Boost called for Harold about five o'clock in the afternoon and they set out for Camberwell together. Mr Boost was silent and moody, replying to Harold's advances by grunts or monosyllables. Harold rather welcomed this attitude on his part than otherwise. It augured well for home-truths at Mr Samuel's shop, and truth was what he particularly desired. The angrier became the protagonists, the more likely he was to learn the true facts about that mysterious bale. For by now he had come to the conclusion that Mr Samuels and his nephew Isidore were far too slippery customers for him to tackle single-handed.

It was dark when they got off the tram, a darkness intensified by a thin mist-like drizzle of rain. As they started to trudge towards Inkerman Street, a fire-engine flashed past them, a whirlwind of bright lights and clanging bells. The traffic drew aside like the waters of the Red Sea at its coming, then surged back to resume its dull and roaring way. Somewhere ahead of them a pulsating glow illumined a fragment of the weeping sky.

'That fire's not far off,' opined Mr Boost. 'All the better; it'll draw most of the folk after it. I'm not anxious to be seen messing about here.'

'Looks like it,' agreed Harold. 'It can't be far beyond Inkerman Street, by the look of it.'

Men passed them running, calling out to one another in raucous cries. Evidently a good fire was regarded as a free entertainment. On either hand small shopkeepers could be seen putting up their shutters hurriedly, and hastening after the throng. The wet breath of the wind carried towards them a sharp and acrid tang of burning.

Mr Boost and Harold quickened their steps, half uncon-sciously; such is the power of crowd-psychosis. Jostled by the throng, they reached the end of Inkerman Street and, as they did so, the full glare of the conflagration burst upon them. Halfway down the narrow thoroughfare a cordon of police, black figures against a sea of light, held at bay a seething mass of sightseers. Beyond them a couple of fire-engines, their polished brass reflecting the red fury of the flames, poured steady streams of water upon a house through whose roof angry tongues were already licking.

Mr Boost rapped out an oath and caught Harold by the arm. 'That's Samuels' place a-burning!' he exclaimed. 'Damned if I don't believe the comrades have paid him back after all! Blasted fools! He'll laugh like hell at it. I'll bet he's insured himself for four times the value of the stuff. I wonder where he's got to!'

'By Jove,' replied Harold. 'What if he was in bed in that back room still? There wouldn't be much left of him by this time!'

Mr Boost laughed, shortly and scornfully. 'Old Samuels let himself be caught like that, eh?' he said. 'No fear, he's too cunning an old swine for that. Come on! Let's get as close as we can and find out.'

He threw his weight into the fray, and, ably assisted by Harold, the two fought their way amid a storm of objurgation through the serried ranks towards the cordon of police. They had nearly achieved their aim, when Mr Boost suddenly sheered off, followed by Harold, and elbowed his way towards a little man in a tattered overcoat, who was dancing about on tiptoe, vainly trying to get a view of the spectacle.

Mr Boost laid a heavy hand upon his shoulder. The little man started, as though betrayed by an uneasy conscience. He turned sharply and peered up into Mr Boost's face.

'Oh, it's you, comrade, is it?' he exclaimed in tones of mani-fest relief. 'You gave me a regular start, you did, coming on a fellow like that. You've got business over yonder, maybe?'

'Never you mind what my business is, Bob,' replied Mr Boost. 'You're just the man I want to see. I want to know how this happened. No lies, now, it's the truth I'm after.'

Bob became voluble at once. 'I wouldn't tell you no lies, comrade, you know that,' he protested. 'And it's the truth I don't know how it happened, s' help me, Dick. Just burst into flames, the old place did, not more'n an hour ago. I see'd the old man leave the place, and then his nevvy rushed out hollerin' . . .'

He broke off shortly, suddenly becoming aware of Harold's interested face at Mr Boost's side.

''Oo's this?' he whispered hoarsely. 'You didn't ought to come up to me in a crowd like this. You can't never tell who's listenin'.'

'Well, come out of it,' replied Mr Boost impatiently, grasping him firmly by the arm. 'This chap's all right. He came along o' me. Now then, Bob, step lively.'

Thus adjured, and impelled by Mr Boost's powerful arm, Bob wormed his way through the crowd to a portion of the pavement more remote from the fire and comparatively clear from sightseers. Once there, he turned complainingly to Mr Boost.

'Oh dear! Oh dear! You'll be the death of me, comrade,' he moaned. 'Why can't you let a fellow alone? Near broke my arm, you did, with that great fist o' yourn.'

'Oh, stow it, Bob,' interrupted Mr Boost. 'What's all this about the old man and Isidore? Where are they? I want a word with 'em, sharp.'

'Isidore's safe enough,' replied Bob with a malicious grin. 'I got my eye on him all right. But the old man's gone, like the wily old devil he is. 'Tain't like him to hang about to be asked awkward questions. Oh, he's a cunning old cuss, he is.'

'Gone?' said Mr Boost. 'Where the devil's he gone to? What yer mean, gone?'

'Well, I'm telling yer, ain't I?' replied Bob, plaintively. 'I saw 'im go, and I 'eard 'im tell the cabby to drive to Waterloo Station.'

'What cabby? When did he go then?' inquired Mr Boost.

'Why, the cabby what came to fetch 'im,' replied Bob. ''Bout three o'clock it must have been. I was standing at the door of my 'ouse, when a four-wheeled cab comes along and draws up outside the old man's shop.

'"'Ullo!" thinks I, "that'll be a customer!" Then I looks for some fun. The old man don't open the door to anybody. He's been ill or something for two or three weeks now, and the door's never opened till that nevvy of 'is comes 'ome. Well, the cabby climbs down from his box, and raps at the door. Knock away, my lad, thinks I. Your knuckles'll be sore before you're finished with that game. But not a bit of it. Cabby hadn't knocked above a couple of times when the door opens, and the old man hobbles out, all muffled-up like, an' wheezin' an' coughin' like you've 'eard 'im a score o' times, only worse. 'E looked fit to drop, an' I thought 'e'd never manage to get into the cab. 'Owever, cabby gives 'im 'is arm, and between 'em 'e gets into the cab somehow. 'E coughs and grumbles for a bit, then he manages to growl out, "Waterloo Station, an' look sharp." The cab drives away, an' that's the last I see of 'im.'

'Gone to have a holiday in the country, I suppose,' commented Mr Boost scornfully. 'But what about Isidore? He hadn't come back, I suppose?'

'I dunno,' replied Bob. 'I didn't see 'im, not then, that is. 'E can't 'ave been in, 'cos the old man locked the door behind 'im when 'e came out an' put the key in 'is pocket. I see'd 'im do it. It warn't till 'e came rushin' out—'

'Yes, yes, but what 'appened next?' interrupted Mr Boost.

'Why, Bill Watters, wot lives up the road, comes up to me and says, "The old man don't look too grand, does 'e?" He'd seen 'im go off, too. We 'as a bit of a yarn, then I goes back into my 'ouse and lies down for a sleep. Next thing I 'eard was a lot of 'ollerin' down the road, and chaps runnin' like mad. So I comes out, and sees a crowd standin' round the old man's shop, a-starin' at the windows. Sure enough there was a lot of smoke comin' out of all of 'em. Then I guessed what 'ad 'appened, and why the old man 'ad made off. Well, I thinks, there's a lot o' junk in there that won't be any the worse for burnin', when all of a sudden I sees the shop window flung up and out tumbles that there nevvy, with nothing on but a shirt and a pair o' socks. Would you believe it, that murderin' old devil 'ad left 'im there to burn!'

Bob paused, gratified at the dramatic climax of his recital. But Mr Boost was wholly unimpressed.

'Well, get on!' he exclaimed impatiently. 'What became of Isidore, then?'

'Why, you know 'e was always a bit soft, like,' replied Bob. 'The fire seems to 'ave sent 'im quite balmy. 'E sprawls about on the pavement, a most disgustin' sight, 'ollerin', "'Elp, 'elp! Fire, fire!" as though anyone couldn't see that the place was alight. Nobody seems to know what to do, so I lays 'old of 'im. "'Ere, you come along o' me, young feller," I says. "You ought to be ashamed o' yourself, that you did, with ladies about an' all." So with that I lugs 'im up and takes 'im 'ome to my place. He sort o' went off like when I gets 'im there, so I shoves 'im on a bed, and there 'e is. Like to 'ave a look at 'im?'

Mr Boost nodded. 'Best thing you could have done, Bob,' he said. 'Yes, let's go and have a word with him.'

Suiting the action to the word, Mr Boost put his powerful elbows into action again, and, closely followed by Harold and Bob, forced a passage through the crowd until they reached the door of one of the dilapidated houses towards the end of Inkerman Street remote from the fire. They followed Bob up a couple of flights of rickety steps, and paused before a closed door.

''E's in there,' exclaimed Bob, in a husky whisper. 'Proper done in 'e is, too.'

'Well, we'll see if we can't get some sense into him,' replied Mr Boost grimly, laying his hand on the door and flinging it open.

There was no lamp in the room, but the glare of the fire outside illuminated it with a red flickering glow. It held a few crazy sticks of furniture, and a couple of old iron bedsteads, upon which lay in disorder a few stained and discoloured blankets. But of any human occupant there was no sign.

Bob looked once round the room and dropped his jaw in dismay. 'Why, 'e's gorn!' he exclaimed.

'Gone? What the devil do you mean?' replied Mr Boost angrily. 'Look here, Bob, none o' your games with me. You know it won't do.'

'S'help me, I ain't told you nothing but the truth, comrade,' asserted Bob plaintively. 'I left 'im 'ere and then went off to see the engines come, and then I stays till you comes up.'

Mr Boost looked at him threateningly. Despite the duplicity written large all over the man, there was an unmistakable note of sincerity in his tones.

'If he only had his shirt and socks on, he can't have gone very far,' said Mr Boost decisively. 'He's probably in the house somewhere.' He turned to Harold. 'Come on, we'll have a look for the young fellow.'

They had scarcely descended more than a few stairs when a bitter howl from Bob arrested them.

'What's up now?' exclaimed Mr Boost. He and Harold rushed back into the room, to find Bob executing a fantastic war-dance, shaking both fists in the air the while.

''E's gorn, I told yer 'e'd gorn!' he exclaimed as soon as he caught sight of Mr Boost. 'The artful young dodger! 'E's taken my Jim's Sunday suit wot was lying on that there chair. Blamed if I know what my Jim'll say when 'e comes 'ome. 'E'll wallop me for sure. O lor, O lor!'

Mr Boost swore angrily. Then, accepting his defeat like a strong man, he shrugged his shoulders and turned to Harold.

'We'd best go home, you and I,' he said. 'We've been properly fooled all along the line. That young rascal must have dressed as soon as Bob's back was turned, and sloped off in the crowd. Might as well look for a needle in a haystack. Come on!'

He and Harold turned to go, heedless of the clamour of the bereaved Bob.

''Ere, what about my Jim's Sunday suit?' he protested wrathfully.

'Damn your Jim's Sunday suit!' replied Mr Boost. 'You ought to have known better than to leave young Isidore alone in here. Why didn't you lock the door?'

And with this parting admonition they left the house and regained the street once more.

The fire was still burning brightly, and it was obvious that Mr Samuels' shop was doomed. Stacked with dry wooden lumber as it was, the flames had got complete command, and the place was alight from cellar to attic. Indeed, the firemen were devoting their efforts to preventing the spread of the conflagration, and one hose only still poured water into the heart of the furnace, which rose in a tower of steam tinged blood-red by the flames beneath.

'I wonder what his game was?' mused Mr Boost, as he and Harold edged their way out of the crowd. 'Looks to me as if he'd fixed it up with young Isidore. He clears out, so that everybody should see him. Then Isidore comes along—there is a back entrance in the next street, though everybody don't know that, and like enough he slips in that way. Everything's all ready. Isidore strikes a match, and when it gets too hot for him, he tumbles out of the window.'

'It looks very much like it,' agreed Harold. 'But why only in his shirt?'

Mr Boost chuckled. 'Cunning young devil!' he replied. 'He must have watched till he saw someone outside who knew him. What else could they do but take him in? He'd be bound to find clothes of some sort, even if they didn't give him any. And he'd be left alone, too, since everyone was sure to run out and watch the fire. Then nothing would be easier than to slip away in the crowd without being recognised.'

'I wonder where he's gone to?' suggested Harold.

'Off to join the old man somewhere, I expect,' replied Mr Boost. 'Samuels will have taken the cash-box with him in the cab and they'll be quite happy even if the insurance people don't pay up. They'll manage to cover their tracks somehow. Old Samuels must have guessed that it was about time he cleared out of the comrades' way. And I'm bound to say he chose a pretty artful way of doing it.'

They were clear of the end of Inkerman Street by this time. As they turned the corner, a taxi drove up, and as it slowed down to avoid the crowd, a woman jumped out, thrust a note into the driver's hand, and began to run towards the fire.

Harold stared at her for an instant. Then he started forward. The woman caught sight of him and stopped with a startled cry. The glow of the fire lit up her face distinctly. It was Vere.

CHAPTER X

VERE and Harold stood as if suddenly turned into stone, staring at one another, unable to find words in which to speak. To each it was inexplicable what the other was doing here, why the glow of a fire in Inkerman Street called them from the ends of London to meet there. And it was Vere who first recovered her presence of mind.

'Harold!' she exclaimed. 'What in the world are you doing here, of all places?'

He hesitated for a moment. After all, what was he doing? He had set out on the faint trail of an elusive clue, but it seemed now that the clue had escaped him for ever. He laughed shortly.

'Well, I came to see the fellow whose shop is now providing that jolly bonfire over there,' he replied. 'My friend here, who happens to be my landlord—'

He turned, as though to introduce Vere and Mr Boost. But Mr Boost was nowhere to be seen. Like a discreet companion, he had slipped away at the appearance of this girl, whose life he shrewdly guessed to be intertwined with Harold's.

Vere turned sharply, and, seeing no one, turned to Harold inquiringly. 'Who was it?' she asked.

'Oh, only Mr Boost,' replied Harold. 'You know the fellow whose shop I live over. He had some business or other with old Samuels, and as I had nothing better to do I came along with him.'

The mention of the name Samuels brought back all the anxiety to Vere's face. She suddenly put out her hand and caught Harold's arm. 'Samuels? What have you got to do with him?' she gasped. 'It *is* his place that's on fire? They told me so at the end of the street, but I wouldn't believe it till I'd seen for myself. I must go—'

She suddenly released Harold's arm, and started off towards the impenetrable wall of the crowd. But Harold grasped her by the wrist and restrained her.

'It's no use, Vere, you can't get near the place,' he said soothingly. 'There's half the population of Camberwell, to say nothing of scores of police and firemen, between us and the fire. Besides, what business is it of yours, anyway?'

'Business?' she flashed at him. 'Business enough, if you knew. Anyway, a jolly sight more business than it is of yours. Let me go.'

Shrugging his shoulders, he dropped her hand obediently. He had experienced her capabilities for making a scene, and he had no desire to become a centre of attraction, second only in interest to the fire itself. Vere started away from him, and by sheer energy succeeded in forcing a way for a few paces through the throng, only to stop discouraged in the centre of a serried knot of people wholly oblivious to her pleadings.

Harold made his way after her and, not without a struggle, succeeded in getting close enough to whisper in her ear.

'It's no good,' he said soothingly, 'You'd much better come away out of it. I know the whole story, if it interests you.'

She turned almost gratefully. 'Harold, dear, I'm so worried,' she replied. 'You don't understand—' A sudden look of fear sprang to her eyes. 'Unless—unless you've found out—'

'I haven't found anything out,' Harold hastened to reassure her. 'I wish I had. But, look here, we can talk somewhere else. Let's get you out of this mob to begin with.'

It was easy enough to get away from the fire, and very soon Vere and Harold found themselves beyond the end of Inkerman Street. Harold remembered that on his way to the tram he had seen a squalid-looking tea-shop, and to this unpromising haven he silently led Vere. It was not until they were seated at a fly-blown marble-topped table that Vere spoke.

'Thank you, Harold dear,' she said simply. 'I am sorry that I lost my temper with you the other night. I was worried, unstrung. You wouldn't understand. Tell me what you know about—about Samuels and his nephew.'

Harold glanced at her in amazement. What on earth could she know about these two? Was it some business connected with them that had brought her post-haste to Camberwell in a taxi? There seemed much to be learned here, if he played his cards properly.

Vere listened attentively while Harold told her the events of the afternoon, as recounted by the voluble Bob. She made no comment until Harold began to elaborate Mr Boost's theory of collusion between the old man and his nephew. But at this she shook her head violently.

'Never!' she exclaimed. 'They hated one another too bitterly for that ever to be possible. No, it's much more likely that old Samuels set a trap for young Isidore. I don't understand it quite, but they are both as cunning as they can be.'

'Hated one another, did they?' said Harold musingly. 'Well, it certainly seemed that young Isidore was afraid of his uncle the last time I saw him—'

'You've seen him!' gasped Vere. 'When, and whatever made you think he was *afraid* of old Samuels?'

'Oh, I'd better tell you the whole story, I suppose,' said Harold. 'I came down here once about a week ago to interview Samuels on Mr Boost's behalf.'

Vere listened to the story of Harold's visit to Samuels' shop, and when he had finished, she sat for some time in silence, playing with her tea-spoon.

'I can't make it out at all,' she said at last. 'You seem to know so much already that you might as well know everything. Listen, and I'll tell you. Old Samuels is a Jew. Nobody quite knows where he comes from, or anything about him. I've been told he came from Budapest some years ago, but I don't know for certain. Since he's been in London, he's been mixed up with all sorts of queer things, and it seems pretty certain that by one means or another he has made a lot of money. He was supposed to be an anarchist or something, but they say he is anything that gives him the chance of making a bit at the moment.'

Harold nodded. So far this tallied with Mr Boost's account of Mr Samuels. 'What is he like to look at?' he enquired.

Vere shuddered. 'Oh, a horrible-looking old man!' she exclaimed. 'All hairy and bedraggled, always muffled up in lots of filthy old clothes, put on one on top of the other. He walks about with a thick stick and coughs and wheezes in a most disgusting way. Sometimes, when he's ill, he's worse than ever. When he first came to England he had a younger sister with him, whom I believe he used to treat abominably. Anyway, she ran away with a Christian who deserted her after a few months. The wretched woman must have had some spirit, for she came back to Samuels and threatened to give away some secret or other of his she had got hold of if he didn't let her live with him peaceably. Samuels gave in and after a short time her child was born. That was Isidore.'

'I see,' replied Harold. 'But what became of his mother?'

'Oh, she died,' said Vere. 'Old Samuels saw to that, I expect. But from the moment of his birth he took a violent hatred to the boy. Of course, it was another mouth to be filled, but there was something more than that. Samuels, disreputable old rascal though he is, always professes to be very strict with regard to his religion. The fact of his sister's lapse did not worry him of itself, but he never stopped sneering and nagging at her for being the mother of a Christian's child. And, unfortunately for the wretched infant, when he was born he happened to have a birth-mark in the form of a cross on his left shoulder.

'His mother said nothing about this, naturally, and, in order to pacify her brother, promised to bring the child up as a Jew. But one day Samuels accidentally caught sight of this mark, and kicked up a frightful fuss. He said it was a judgment upon his sister for her sins, that the child was a scapegoat, born with the mark of the gallows upon it, and I don't know what else. Anyway, the wretched woman died soon afterwards, and the old man promptly got rid of the child, gave someone a few pounds to take it away and never let him see it again. That's how Isidore began life.'

She paused, and Harold, interested despite himself in this queer story, prompted her gently.

'What happened then?' he asked. 'How did the two come together again?'

'It seems that the woman Samuels had paid to take his nephew away had, in her turn, disposed of him to a travelling showman, and eventually lost sight of him. Then, like everybody else, she quarrelled with Samuels, and, looking about for some means of getting even with him, thought of Isidore. She managed to find him, and made it her business to tell him the whole story of his birth, and who his uncle was. By this time he was a lad of eighteen or so, quite of an age to be a considerable thorn in the old man's flesh, if he had wanted to be.'

'I see,' put in Harold. 'And he's been living on the old man ever since. I don't wonder they hate one another.'

But Vere shook her head. 'No, it's not quite so simple as all that,' she replied. 'Isidore isn't by any means the half-witted fool he pretends to be to strangers. He had managed to pick up a certain amount of education in his wanderings, and he was intensely ambitious. He very soon found out what his uncle was worth, and from the first he made up his mind to get hold of the money. He went to see his uncle, told him he was quite ready to help him with the business in the evenings, that he had a job which would keep him in the daytime, and all that sort of thing. Old Samuels, who had no idea how much he knew, but guessed that he knew enough to make things jolly unpleasant for him if he wanted to, was forced to agree.'

Harold smiled. 'I expect he wished him to the devil,' he said. 'But what was the job young Isidore had?'

Vere shook her head. 'I don't know,' she replied. 'It was soon after this I first met him. Oh, don't be alarmed. I'm not going to give you the pathetic history of the early years of the girl who went astray. I kept house not far from here for a drunken father, and that's enough for you to know.

'I wasn't the only girl attracted by young Isidore, but he took to me more than to the others. I'm not denying that he helped me. It was through him that I took lessons in shorthand and typewriting, and so got a job which led to my present one. That was all part of his game.'

A sudden light broke upon Harold. 'Then, why—good Lord, Isidore is the fellow—' he began excitedly.

'Of course,' replied Vere. 'How else do you suppose I knew all this? What did you suppose I was doing in this part of town at all? I had come down here, when I thought I should find him in the evening, to—to tell him that I had broken off with you, and that he could do as he liked for all I cared. I saw that story in *The Weekly Record* yesterday and it gave me an idea. I was furious with you, Harold dear, and I wanted my own back. I was going to pretend that the story was true, that I was the girl, and I wanted him to help me. Then the taxi-man said he couldn't go any further, and I asked a man where the fire was, then I saw you—'

She paused in confusion, looking at him imploringly. But Harold, hot on this new scent, had no eyes for her distress.

'But I don't understand,' he said abruptly. 'You didn't live together. You've got your room in Bloomsbury, and you say that he lived with his uncle here.'

'All part of his game,' she replied. 'As soon as I had a job of my own, he began to work on my gratitude. He wanted money, wanted it badly and I must lend it to him. He made a little for himself, but he wanted more, just a little more, for a few years. Then everything would be all right, and he would pay me back handsomely. If I wouldn't do it he would go to my employers and tell them facts about me which would very soon get me the sack. I was utterly in his hands, you see.

'Well, I had to agree, and this went on for years. I saw him off and on, about once a week, when he came to get what he could out of me. And every time he told me he was getting nearer his goal, that the time was soon coming when he wouldn't trouble me any more. Then came the evening I told you about. You can guess that by this time I was ready to promise anything to get rid of him. You understand why I did it, don't you, Harold, dear?'

'It seems to me it is all a devil of a mess,' replied Harold gloomily. 'The only thing to do is to find Isidore and get the whole truth out of him. You say he told you he had all the money he wanted now? Well, it seems pretty clear he didn't get it from his uncle, for the old man appears to have bolted with the cash this afternoon. He must have got it through that mysterious job of his, which I expect was a partnership in some burglary syndicate, or something of the kind.'

Suddenly he turned upon her eagerly. 'Look here, Vere, you want to find this fellow again, don't you?' he exclaimed.

She looked at him and smiled sadly. 'Yes, I suppose I do,' she agreed. 'I can't go on wondering when he will turn up again to plague me. I must know the truth, once and for all.'

'Well, then, will you tell a friend of mine who is helping to find out about the man I found dead in my rooms, all you've told me?'

She started, and stared at him curiously. 'A friend?' she replied. 'What sort of a friend?'

'An old professor I've known all my life,' answered Harold. 'Come on, we'll go and see him now. He's an awfully kind old chap, and if anybody can help us, he can.'

She rose languidly. 'Yes, it doesn't matter much, I suppose,' she said. 'I can't go on like this; something's got to happen. And I've no friends to help me out.'

It was a silent drive in the taxi that Harold secured. The whole way to Westbourne Terrace each was preoccupied with divergent thoughts, each sought the solution to a different problem, of which Isidore Samuels was the only common factor. The clocks were striking eight as Mary, vastly intrigued at the sight of Vere in Harold's company, showed them into the Professor's study.

They had not long to wait. Professor Priestley joined them within a minute of their arrival. 'Good evening, my boy,' he said as he entered the room. 'This is Miss Donaldson, I presume? Pray take a seat. I am delighted to make your acquaintance.'

He took no further heed of Harold, but devoted himself to Vere, striving to overcome her embarrassment and make her feel at home. 'No, you have not disturbed me in the least,' Harold heard him say. 'As it happens, I am dining alone, and dinner is always a movable feast on such occasions. I am more than delighted that Harold persuaded you to come.'

Harold, for his part, strained his ears for some indication of April's presence in the house, longing to hear if only the echo of her voice, dreading lest she should enter the room and see Vere. He heard the door-bell ring, heard Mary open it and a man's footsteps enter. Then April's voice from the head of the stairs, 'Oh, there you are at last, Evan, you're very late! I've been ready for ages.'

The door opened once more, then shut with a slam. A taxi panted outside, then hummed away into the distance. And Harold, with a sigh, turned to the Professor.

But the latter would have none of him. 'My dear boy,' he said, 'Miss Donaldson tells me that she wishes to ask my advice upon a somewhat delicate matter. She will, I am sure, feel less embarrassed if we are left alone.'

Harold smiled. This at least was definite enough. He took up his hat and walked home to Riverside Gardens, his brain filled with conjectures as to Isidore Samuels and his secret. That there was some connection between this elusive young man and his own problem he was now sure. But—Isidore had disappeared, this time for good, it seemed. And how he was to be traced was more than Harold could imagine.

It was well after midnight when April, returning from her dance, saw, to her surprise, a light in her father's study. She hesitated for a moment, and hearing nothing, opened the door softly and tiptoed in. The Professor was seated in his favourite chair, his eyes fixed intently upon the dying embers of the fire. He started at the sound of her footsteps, and looked at her gravely, almost anxiously.

She came and perched herself on the arm of his chair, then leant over and kissed the top of his head.

'You ought to be in bed long ago, Daddy mine,' she said. 'What are you doing in here all by yourself?'

'Thinking, my dear,' replied the Professor gently. 'Wondering, if you will, if I dare to embark upon the solution of a problem. There are certain mysteries in this world which are better left unsolved.'

'I believe you love your old problems far more than you do your daughter,' she said lightly.

'I see more of them, perhaps,' he replied after a pause. 'It seems to me that young Evan Denbigh has the first claim to your time now.'

She laid her head upon his shoulder and laughed softly. 'I believe you are jealous of Evan, Daddy,' she said. 'I'll stop at home if you like, and do problems with you. We'll evaluate x plus y to the power of n, or something thrilling like that, every evening for an hour after dinner. Won't that be fun?'

But he was not to be put off by her banter. 'Tell me, dear, are you fond of this young man?' he said.

'*On s'amuse*,' she replied carelessly. 'He's interesting to talk to, he dances well, he knows how to behave. You were the first to point out his merits, I believe, Daddy mine.'

'Yes, but do you care for him?' persisted the Professor.

'What an inquisitive old darling it is!' mocked April, and then suddenly her voice changed. 'Oh, he's one of many. What do I care? They're all the same, all good fun to go out with, all to be trusted to behave decently in public. You know quite well, since Harold gave up caring—'

She broke off abruptly, and so for a while they sat, the

Professor tenderly stroking her hand, she with her head resting on his shoulder. Then all of a sudden she kissed him, sprang from the arm of the chair and was gone.

Professor Priestley, left alone, stared reflectively for a few seconds into the fireplace. Then almost reverently he felt with his fingers the shoulder of his coat where his daughter's head had rested. A great thankfulness lit up his face as he found it still moist.

'So it is Harold, after all!' he murmured. 'Thank God! Now I can do my duty.'

CHAPTER XI

EVAN Denbigh was a man who always took particular care as to his personal appearance. His bedroom in Cambridge Terrace was in the greatest contrast to Harold's careless untidiness at Riverside Gardens. It was, perhaps, less ornately furnished, but it was evident that its occupant was of an orderly mind, believing in that proverbial Utopia, a place for everything and everything in its place. He had only recently removed to these rooms, but already his landlady had confided to her friends of similar profession that her new tenant was a real gentleman and one who could be trusted not to muck things about.

On this particular afternoon, a couple of days after the evening when he had been late in calling for April, he was dressing with particular care. Sir Alured Faversham was taking a well-earned holiday, and it was by his own suggestion that his zealous assistant was attending at the laboratory during the mornings only. 'It doesn't do to burn the candle at both ends at your age, Denbigh,' he had said kindly. 'You've been looking a bit tired lately. There won't be much doing while I am away, and it'll be quite good enough if you come here in the mornings. Have your afternoons to yourself and take things easily.'

Evan had thanked him warmly, and had delicately conveyed the intelligence to April. As he had hoped, he had been rewarded by an invitation to tea on the Wednesday, and it was for this particular function that he was now preparing. For, with any luck, it would mean a *tête-à-tête* with April, and of that interview he was resolved to take the fullest advantage. It seemed to him that the hour for which he had been waiting had struck at last. Surely there had been something in her manner the other evening which had implied encouragement! Come what might, he would put it to the test this very afternoon.

With that intention in his mind his toilet was more elaborate than usual. As he put the finishing touches, he considered very carefully what his exact course should be. He had received a note from April herself, couched in the usual careless phraseology she habitually adopted. 'If you haven't anything more interesting on, come round to tea and talk.' Just that, but quite enough to make a heart beat faster with gladness at an unsought, a heaven-sent opportunity. Tea and talk! Rather! As if there could be anything more interesting.

Of course, it must be quite a family affair, just April and the Professor, with the vague chance of some other casual visitor. He must risk that; in any case there might be no difficulty. The Professor always went off to his study directly after tea, and if the visitor was for him, he would go, too, leaving the field clear. Visitors for April? Well, that would mean Fabian tactics, a game of inducing the other fellow to go first. But really there was little to fear in that direction. The only man he had ever suspected April of having any regard for was Harold Merefield. And poor Harold's stock was a bit low with that cloud that hung over him, and suspicion newly awakened by the letter in *The Weekly Record*. There was nothing to fear in that direction.

Then what would happen next? Opportunity was all very well, but how to seize it? How to make the most of the chance that fate had thrown into his way? April and he were excellent friends, there could be no doubt of that; they had common tastes, they had seen quite a lot of one another lately, to her manifest enjoyment. Yet somehow there was a great gulf fixed, the mist-shaded gulf that lies between friendship and—something more. You came to the end of friendship, as he had, deliberately, stepping carefully. Beyond, across the gulf, usually hidden by the mist, but sometimes half revealed in a sudden eddy, lay the further shore, the goal of all your efforts. And in between lay the dark ravine in which there seemed no foothold.

You had to bridge that gulf, bridge it with such frail materials as lay to your hands or as the gods might send. A flimsy, crazy structure when you had built it, a gossamer-thread of a thing, which the first breath of resentment, of indifference, of ridicule, would utterly sweep away. And you must fall with it, tumble head over heels into the gulf itself, without hope of scaling its steep sides to either shore, that of friendship or of love. You took your ambitions with you when you set out to cross that bridge. If it failed, they failed with it.

So Evan Denbigh, brush in hand, thought as he flicked the last speck of dust from his coat. A desperate venture, perhaps, but he meant to risk it. Surely he had read encouragement in her manner, as much encouragement as the off-hand, ultra-modern April could be expected to hold out. Besides, he would build the approaches carefully, set up the foundations of his arch in her sight, the while he remained safely on firm land. He could trust himself to use infinite pains, infinite caution—.

He was ready at last, and with a bold heart he set out for Westbourne Terrace. He walked slowly, consulting his watch every few paces, curbing his eagerness with a resolve to arrive exactly at the appointed hour. Even so, he was too early, was compelled to follow a tortuous route, past the busy importance of Paddington Station, into the long avenue of his goal, already darkening with the approach of the winter evening. At last a near-by clock chimed the quarters, and with a racing pulse he mounted the front-door steps and rang the bell.

Mary let him in, with a smile she reserved for those of whom she approved. Failing Master Harold—and after all the dreadful things they said, it seemed that Master Harold was no longer in the race—this spruce, pleasant-spoken young man seemed to answer her intuitive tests. She was about to show him upstairs to the drawing-room, when the Professor bustled out of his study and nearly ran into him.

'Ah, Denbigh, so it is you, is it?' he said. 'Dear me, that is very fortunate. Come in. I daresay you will be very interested in some figures I am working upon. I flatter myself that they will completely upset the accepted theory of the structure of the atom. Facts, Denbigh, facts, as opposed to mere conjecture. Come in and I will explain them to you.'

There was nothing for it. Denbigh obediently followed Professor Priestley into his study, with a mental prayer that Mary would announce his arrival to April, who would organise an expedition to rescue him. Meanwhile he determined to make himself pleasant to the old man. He fully recognised the importance of making sure of this important ally.

The study was in darkness, save for a single lamp resting on a folding table spread out in the centre of the room. On that table lay an enormous sheet of squared paper, on which were inscribed rows of neat figures, and a sheaf of graphs, traced in many-coloured chalks, looking like the tracks of so many rockets. By the side of the paper was an array of mathematical instruments of various kinds, pencils and other aids to draughtsmanship.

The Professor led the way up to the table, talking as he did so. 'I have never been prepared to accept the radioactive theory of the construction of matter,' he said. 'I know you chemists have constructed a theory of the atom as a miniature solar system, with electrons wandering about in it like planets. Pure conjecture, nothing logical about it. In the first place, you have never seen an atom, have you?'

'No, I must confess I haven't,' replied Denbigh, cautiously feeling his way. 'But men like Rutherford—'

'Inference, experimental inference, if you like, but still inference,' interrupted the Professor. 'Now, for my part, I can prove mathematically, logically, and therefore conclusively, that your much-vaunted atomic structure is impossible. The laws of mutual attraction do not admit of it.'

He picked up a pencil, and laid the point of it on his chart. 'Now, follow this curve,' he continued excitedly. 'It shows the mutual attraction of two particles of given mass as the distance increases. You see, at this critical point, as we may call it—ah, bother it!'

The fine point of the pencil had broken beneath his pressure, and as he continued his explanation he picked up a penknife and began to resharpen it, regardless of the luxurious carpet which covered the floor.

'At this critical point, the curve becomes to all intents and purposes parallel to its abscissæ. You see what that means? It means that when your particles diverge beyond that distance, there is practically no force tending to hold them together. Ah, that is better!'

The pencil was now sharpened to his liking, and he reached over the table to lay it down. In doing so his arm caught the edge of it, and it tilted perilously. An avalanche of rulers, dividers, and a thousand queer-shaped things began to roll over it, and both the Professor and Denbigh, who stood by his side, made a sudden grab to arrest them. Denbigh, as he did so, gave a sudden exclamation. The Professor, in his flurry, had driven the point of his penknife into his arm.

'Good gracious!' exclaimed the latter, as he realised what had happened. 'How extremely clumsy of me! One should never hold an open knife in one's hand! And, dear me, I have been sharpening coloured pencils with this one! How unfortunate; it may set up serious irritation. I must attend to it directly!'

'Oh, it's nothing,' replied Denbigh laughingly. 'The point hardly penetrated the skin. Really, it isn't worth while making a fuss about.'

But the Professor shook his head, and pressed the electric bell by the side of the fireplace. 'I am surprised at one of your profession treating a matter of this kind so lightly,' he remarked, severely. 'It is inattention to such details which is responsible for so many cases of blood-poisoning. The dye used to colour these pencils has a definitely toxic action—'

The entrance of Mary in response to his ringing checked the flow of his eloquence. 'Ah, Mary!' he said, turning to her, 'will you please go upstairs to Miss April and ask her to come down to me with the first-aid case which she will find in the cupboard at the head of my bed? Thank you.'

Denbigh's reluctance disappeared as if by magic. 'Yes, perhaps you're right,' he said, as Mary left the room on her errand. 'You never know how small a thing will give rise to sepsis. A touch of iodine might be a good thing, after all.'

He stopped as he heard April running down the staircase and bowed smilingly as she burst open the door. This little incident had saved him a somewhat boring quarter of an hour. Now the spell was broken—after tea his opportunity must come—

'What have you two been up to?' demanded April. 'Mary came up and said you wanted the first-aid things at once. Who's the patient?'

'My dear, I have had the misfortune to inflict a slight stab with my penknife upon Denbigh's arm,' replied the Professor. 'You are aware how dangerous such a superficial wound may prove. You have the iodine and a bandage? Excellent! Now, Denbigh, if you will remove your coat and roll up your shirt sleeve, my daughter, whose sight is better than mine, will attend to you.'

Denbigh did as he was told, but his half-reluctant efforts failed to meet with the Professor's approval. The wound was well up in the left biceps, a trifling incision from the lips of which a drop of blood oozed slowly.

'Roll your sleeve right up,' commanded the Professor. 'April will want to apply plenty of iodine, and it produces an indelible stain on linen. Ah, that's better. I think you will hardly need my assistance, my dear.'

'Oh, no, that's all right, Daddy,' replied April, as the Professor turned to the disordered table and began to gather up his scattered instruments. 'This is my job.'

She laid her hands on Denbigh's shirt with a professional touch, and rolled the sleeve well back to the shoulder. 'You didn't know that I meant to be a V.A.D., only the war ended too soon, did you, Evan?' she said. 'How you and father came to stick knives into one another I can't imagine. Now for the iodine. Smart a bit? Of course it does. That's what it's for. Now a couple of turns of bandage, *and* a safety pin, and there's one more patient saved from the horrors of lock-jaw. That's right.'

Denbigh submitted with good grace to her ministrations. The touch of her fingers was very pleasant, the incident somehow made another link between them, provided yet another slender spar for that bridge which was yet to be built. April completed her bandaging, then turned to help her father to collect the various instruments which had fallen to the floor unheeded.

'What on earth were you up to, Daddy dear?' she asked. 'Fencing with pocket-knives, or something like that?'

'No, my dear,' replied the Professor. 'We were seeking facts, when a careless gesture of mine very nearly upset the table, and in trying to save it I wounded Denbigh.'

He turned to the young man, who was putting on his coat. 'You see, as I was about to explain when that unfortunate incident occurred, the curve of mutual attraction—'

But April interrupted him. 'Oh, do give your old curves a rest, Daddy dear!' she exclaimed. 'It's past tea-time already, and you know how cross Mary gets if meals are kept waiting. Come along, I'll help you tidy up this litter.'

The chart was rolled up, and put safely away in a corner, the table upon which it rested was folded up and likewise put away. The Professor himself deposited each of his beloved instruments in its appointed place. Then and not till then would he consent to leave the room, and the three ascended the stairs to the drawing room. With a thrill of excitement, Denbigh realised that opportunity, the opportunity he so eagerly sought for, was drawing nigh.

CHAPTER XII

TEA, but for the Professor, might have proved a somewhat constrained meal. Denbigh, for his part, found it very difficult to appear unconcerned. He was constantly on the alert, dreading lest the door should open to admit further visitors, and so spoil his chances for a *tête-à-tête* with April, when the Professor should have gone back to the study. April, woman-like, displayed no signs of noticing any mental tension in the air, even if she were aware of it.

But the Professor, having once started on his hobby, refused to be diverted from it. His researches into the structure of the atom seemed to afford him enormous satisfaction, and the presence of Denbigh, equipped with a scientific education and so capable of understanding him, was an opportunity not to be lost. He dropped easily into his lecturing style, and proceeded from a consideration of the present case to his favourite theory that mathematics, the logic of facts, was the sole legitimate route to the solution of any possible problem.

April and Denbigh let him talk; indeed, there was no stopping him. But it was with a feeling of devout thankfulness that Denbigh saw him rise, shortly after the assimilation of his second cup of tea.

'This has been a most interesting conversation,' remarked the Professor genially. 'It is not often that I meet one so able to appreciate my theories as you, Denbigh. Most interesting. In fact, I see no reason why it should terminate now. There is an admirable fire in my study, and I find it more comfortable to sit in than this room. Come along, Denbigh, and you too, April, my dear. We will make ourselves comfortable down there.'

For one wild second the thought of rebellion flashed through

Denbigh's mind. This was intolerable. How on earth was he to listen patiently to this old bore and watch the precious minutes slipping by? Once in the study, there would be no chance of securing that longed-for interview with April. There would be nothing for it but to sit on and on, until the inevitable time for his departure came.

But there was no help for it. April had already risen to follow her father, and Denbigh trailed after them, fury in his heart and a smile on his lips. The Professor sank with a sigh into his favourite chair in front of his desk. April dropped on to a cushion before the fire.

'Here you are, Denbigh,' said the Professor, pointing to a sofa against the wall furthest from the door, and separated from the rest of the room by the big desk. 'I can hear you better on my left side. One has to arrange these things at my time of life. April dear, turn out the lights, if you please? It is just as easy to talk in the dark, and I confess that I find the glare of these modern electric lights rather trying. Ah, thank you!'

The study was thus left in comparative darkness. A heavily-shaded lamp on the Professor's desk cast a bright circle of light upon the writing pad, but hardly penetrated the shadows beyond. A couple of big logs in the grate burned redly upon a carefully prepared bed of coal, but their occasional flames did little beyond casting a flickering, uncertain light upon the book-cases that lined the walls. It was, as April remarked, the ideal setting for professorial discussion.

Denbigh acquiesced in the arrangement with a certain fatalism. Since all chance of seeing April alone seemed to have been denied him, he might as well submit to fate and employ his time earning the good opinion of her father. After all, this was merely a postponement; it ought to be easy for him to bring about another opportunity in a day or two. Meanwhile he schooled himself to listen attentively to the Professor's exordium.

But the three had hardly settled themselves before the door opened and Mary appeared, silhouetted against the comparative brightness of the hall. 'Mr Merefield, sir,' she announced, and Harold walked in, blinded by the unaccustomed gloom.

'Ah, Harold, my boy, is that you?' said the Professor equably. 'There is no need for any of us to disturb ourselves. You will find a chair in front of the fire, close to where April is sitting. That's right. I was explaining to Denbigh that the study of facts, if intelligently conducted, is capable of solving any problem which can confront the human brain.'

'Can it, sir?' said Harold with a touch of bitterness in his voice. He had received a note from the Professor asking him to come and see him at five o'clock that evening. Eagerly, feeling that something must have happened to throw a light upon the shadow that enwrapped him, he had hastened to the interview, only to find the Professor, Denbigh, and April sitting in what looked uncommonly like a family circle.

'Yes, it can,' replied the Professor. 'Take your own case, for example. You were the victim of circumstances, of which hitherto it has been very difficult to trace the cause. But I have every reason to hope that by careful recognition of the facts, and the rejection of mere inference, it will be possible to reconstruct the truth.'

'You don't mean to say that you know what happened on that horrible night, do you, Daddy?' exclaimed April. 'It would be splendid if you could show how unfair everybody had been to poor Harold!'

'I may say that I think we can arrive at the truth,' replied the Professor oracularly. 'The attempt will, in any case, form an admirable example of the methods which should be employed in such a case. You all know the general facts of the case, together with the mass of irrelevant matter which threatens to smother them. The only skill required is to detect the facts, to choose the precious metal, as it were, and to reject the dross.'

The Professor paused for a moment, as though to collect his thoughts. His audience made no sign, each feeling that a light was to be thrown at length upon the famous Paddington Mystery.

'Now, my first point is this,' he continued. 'Stripped of infer-ence, there is only one main fact we can rely upon in the discovery of a dead body on Harold's bed. We are forced to conclude that the man reached the position in which he was found through human agency, that he was not propelled there by the force of an explosion or any phenomenon of nature. Therefore, an entry was made into Harold's rooms that night, or rather between the time of his departure, about four o'clock, and the time of his arrival, about three o'clock next morning.

'An examination of the surroundings suggested that someone—and circumstances pointed to that someone being the dead man—had reached the canal bank from Great Western Road, swum the canal, crossed the waste land, and prised up the window of Harold's bedroom with a tyre-lever. This, you will remember, was the view adopted by the police. The tracks of such an event were clearly visible. The dead man's boots fitted the footprints on the waste land exactly, the tyre-lever found in his pocket corresponded exactly with the marks on the window-sash. Indeed, I am myself of opinion that the prints were made by those very boots, and the marks on the window-sash by that identical tyre-lever. I say merely of the opinion, for I have no incontrovertible proof to support that view. It is possible that exactly similar boots and tyre-levers exist. Indeed, as regards the tyre-lever, I know such to be the case.'

'Then are you inclined to agree with Inspector Hanslet's view of the case?' suggested Denbigh.

'Not entirely,' replied the Professor. 'I was struck by the fact that the tyre-lever was an insignificant tool with which to force open a well-made window, securely hasped. Have you had that window repaired, Harold?'

'No, I haven't,' replied Harold. 'I thought it best to leave everything alone for the present.'

'Then the facts which I shall proceed to relate can be veri-fied, if necessary,' said the Professor. 'Now, the police witnesses at the inquest explained that when the window was forced open, the hasp was not broken, but yielded through the screws which secured it withdrawing from the wood. This fact I verified for myself. But there was a further fact, overlooked in the shadow of preconceived inference. When a screw is forcibly torn from wood, the threads of it are clogged with wood fibre. In this case, although each screw was an inch and a half long, only the last quarter of an inch was clogged.'

'By Jove!' exclaimed Harold. 'I never noticed that.'

'Nor, apparently, did Inspector Hanslet,' replied the Professor. 'However, to proceed. My inspection of the wood of the window-frame convinced me that it was in perfectly sound condition. Further, the heads of the screws showed signs of a screw-driver having recently been used upon them. I have no hesitation, therefore, in deducing that, at the time the window was forced, the screws securing the hasp had already been partially withdrawn. Now this would not fail to have been noticed by anyone securing the window with a hasp. Did you do this before you went out that evening, Harold?'

'I did, sir,' replied Harold, 'and I am quite certain the hasp was in order then.'

'You see, now, how significant the apparently insignificant fact has become,' continued the Professor. 'The screws could not be tampered with from outside the window. Yet, on the other hand, there is very little doubt that the window was actually forced from outside, when the hasp had already been sufficiently weakened to enable the window to be prised open with the tyre-lever. We are thus forced to the conclusion that there were at least two separate entries into Harold's rooms that night, one through the window and a previous one through some other means of access. In the absence of any evidence to the contrary, I am inclined to assume for the present that this first means of access was the door, opened in the ordinary way by a key.'

'But nobody else besides me has a key, sir!' put in Harold. 'And I am quite sure that I locked the door behind me.'

The Professor shook his head impatiently. 'Nobody who has a lease of premises can make such an assertion,' he replied. 'Unless he has actually had a lock fitted himself, and even then the statement can only be accepted with reservations. I have no doubt that the conditions are the same in your case as in a thousand others, my own included. The tenant signs a lease, the landlord hands over a key or keys which fit the existing lock. How does the tenant know that he has the only keys which fit that lock? However, I do not wish to stress that point for the moment. I wish to make it clear that some means of access to the rooms existed, other than the window, since we have irrefutable evidence that such an entry was made.'

'Daddy dear, you're a marvel!' exclaimed April. 'Go on, this is most thrilling. What happened next?'

'Not so fast, my dear,' replied the Professor. 'Let us consider for a moment who it was that effected this first entry. Now, abandoning for a moment the actual examination of facts, let us form a theory which we can test later. We have, to begin with, an apparent lack of motive for either entry, of the dead man's presence in the room at all. It is unusual for a man to break into a stranger's rooms for the express purpose of dying on his bed. There seem to me to be two alternatives. One is that the dead man effected both entries, and was overtaken by death before he was able to carry out his purpose. The second is that this man had an accomplice, who decamped as soon as he realised the fate that had overtaken his comrade.

'The second of the possibilities appears to me to be most likely. If the man was alone, I find it difficult to account for his actions. For it is obvious that, when he had already obtained access to the rooms, he deliberately laid a trail, with his own feet and his own tools, by a route involving considerable difficulties, including swimming a canal and climbing at least two walls, and also the risk of observation. If, on the other hand, there were two men involved, it is more understandable that the first gained access to the rooms by the door, and the second by the window. This suggests that the tracks found by the police were deliberately made, for if one man could enter by the door, two could do so with equal ease. Again, why unscrew the fastenings of the hasp and then prise the window open? It would have been simpler, safer and quicker for the first man to have opened the window in the ordinary way for his comrade, supposing, for some reason that we have not yet ascertained, that it was necessary for that comrade to approach the rooms by that route. No, I am convinced that all the tracks subsequently found, the footsteps, the marks on the window, the tyre-lever in the dead man's pocket, the wetness of the clothes, suggesting that he had swum the canal, were all of them made with the intention of their being seen and recognised.'

The Professor paused. His listeners, intent upon his recital, were silent for a moment. Then Harold, who had been following every word with the greatest eagerness, ventured to speak.

'But why, sir?' he asked. 'Why leave these deliberate tracks, I mean? I can understand the man making misleading tracks to hide the way in which he got in, but not, as you put it, with his own tools and his own boots. If he had got away, it would, at least, have given the police a clue to start on. And it seems to me, if he got in by the door, he could have got out by the same way and left no tracks whatever.'

'Exactly!' replied the Professor. 'That is the very point which has interested me from the first. *If he had made his escape.* But suppose for a moment that it was never intended that he should make his escape. What then?'

Denbigh from the sofa gave a slightly depreciating laugh. 'But surely, Professor, you are asking us to assume too much. Followed to a logical conclusion, your suggestion that the man was never intended to escape implies that his accomplice murdered him in Merefield's rooms. But you will remember that there was no trace whatever of a crime or even of a struggle. The man died from heart failure, there is very little doubt of that. I know your mistrust of medical evidence, but, speaking as a doctor, I am satisfied with the jury's verdict. And it can hardly be assumed that the accomplice, whoever he was, could predict that the man would die then, even as a result of the physical strain involved in climbing walls and swimming canals.'

The Professor nodded. 'Thank you, Denbigh, you have exactly voiced the objections which I formed in my own mind. Do not imagine that I reject the medical evidence or the jury's finding. I accept both freely, with limitations. The man died of failure of the heart's action, undoubtedly. But, when, and under what circumstances? That the medical evidence is unable to tell us. The expert witnesses tell us that he died probably during the afternoon preceding the early morning in which he was found. Circumstantial evidence points to his having broken into Harold's rooms between about five p.m. and two a.m. Hence the inference that he died there. But let me put another possibility before you. What if he were already dead when he arrived at Riverside Gardens?'

There was a universal gasp of astonishment, then April laughed outright. 'Daddy dear, you give me the creeps!' she complained. 'You aren't going to suggest that his ghost made those tracks—they were his own boots; you have admitted that yourself.'

'Besides, sir, you can't wander about with a dead body, even in Riverside Gardens,' put in Harold. 'And the man's clothing was soaked with filthy water. It doesn't seem possible that he was put into the canal and then dragged in through my window. And there was no trace of any mess on the stairs.'

'I will deal with your objections first,' replied the Professor patiently. 'We have, I think, established the probability of an accomplice, or second man, being connected with the matter. We have now to consider the probability of this man having, first, a dead body to dispose of, and, second, a means of access to Harold's rooms. It occurs to him that he can use the second as a means to the first. By some means, which I will deal with later, he conveys the body to the front of Mr Boost's house, lets himself in, and deposits the body on Harold's bed. He has now before him the necessity of providing a plausible reason for the presence of that body, of leaving tracks which will lead the opinion of the police and of the public in an entirely wrong direction. I do not, of course, believe for a moment that his action was taken on the spur of the moment; every detail shows evidence of long premeditation.

'He has already provided himself with a screw-driver and a tyre-lever. The first thing he does is to loosen the screws of the hasp, as I have already described. The next thing he does is to leave Harold's rooms in the way he came. The absence of foot-marks on the stairs is no objection to this theory; Mr Boost's front garden is littered with mats and scraps of canvas with which he could have cleaned his boots adequately before entering. Now comes the only dangerous part of his exploit, and in this the foggy nature of the evening favours him. I am even inclined to believe that he waited for a foggy period to fulfil his purpose.'

'But the man can only have died that evening,' objected Denbigh. 'He can't—'

'Oh, shut up, Evan!' interrupted April. 'Don't spoil the story. Proceed, Professor Sherlock Priestley!'

'Well, we will consider Denbigh's objection later,' said the Professor. 'Aided by the fog, the second man, as we will call him, walks straight round to the bridge where the canal crosses the road. Waiting for an opportunity when there are no passers-by, he climbs over the parapet, following the route suggested by Inspector Hanslet, and so reaches the towing path. From there he wades into the canal, swims across, climbs the wall of the courtyard on to the sloping roof below Harold's window, and forces the latter open with the tyre-lever. His task is now finished. All he has to do is to change clothes and boots with the dead man, leave the tyre-lever but not the screw-driver in his pocket, and retire quietly by the front door. An ingenious scheme, and very fascinating in its simplicity.'

'Good Lord!' said Harold. 'I never thought of all that. But what about the other things found in the dead man's pockets, the washers, and so forth?'

'All easily procurable trifles, put there for the express purpose of setting any enquiry on the wrong scent,' replied the Professor. 'This second man took every care to render identification as difficult as possible, realising, no doubt, that such identification would furnish a clue to his own identity.'

The Professor paused, and then turned towards Denbigh. 'What do you think of my theory now?' he enquired with a touch of triumph.

'It's most plausible,' confessed the young man. 'But even so, we are not much further. We don't know who the dead man was, and there is no possible clue to this mysterious second man.'

'Perhaps not, at present,' replied the Professor. 'But if my theory is correct, we have at least established Harold's innocence in the matter.'

'Unless we assume that he had lent the man the keys of his rooms, that evening,' put in April lightly. 'That seems to me to be one of the weak points of your argument, Daddy. Besides, how did the man get the body to Riverside Gardens? He can hardly have driven it there in a taxi.'

'If I am not greatly mistaken, the body was already there when he arrived,' replied the Professor quietly.

'Already there!' exclaimed Harold. 'No, that it can't have been. Yet, by Jove! Mr Boost's missing bale!'

'Of course, of course!' assented the Professor. 'That bale had struck me as an admirable temporary receptacle for a dead body from the very moment I heard of it. But in order that it should have any significance in the present case it was necessary to establish the fact that the man Harold found was dead, or, at least, insensible, before he reached Harold's room. It was also necessary to account for the tracks the police found. One cannot accept some of the facts of a series and ignore the rest. I believe that the body actually reached Riverside Gardens in that bale. You observe what an admirably chosen means of conveyance this was. The second man no doubt arranged for the delivery of this bale on an evening chosen during the time when Mr Boost was absent. It is delivered after Harold leaves his rooms, and all trace of it is removed before his return. Here again the matter is simple. The wrappings of the bale could be flung into Mr Boost's front garden without attracting attention among the rest of the litter lying there. The fact that the bale had ever existed was not likely to come to light until Mr Boost returned to his shop, at the earliest. As it turned out, it was only through the accident of Mr Boost having business with George, the carter, that he became aware of the delivery of the bale as early as he did.'

'But, Professor, this is pure conjecture!' exclaimed Denbigh. 'I gather that a bale of some kind, which might have contained a body, is said to have been delivered at Riverside Gardens that evening, and that it is also said to have mysteriously disappeared. I see no facts to connect this bale with the man Merefield found in his rooms.'

'In a matter such as this it is frequently necessary to proceed by the method of trial and error,' replied the Professor gravely. 'In other words, to select theories in turn, and to apply to them the test of known facts, accepting only the one which success-fully survives this test.'

The Professor drew out his watch, and held it in the circle of light thrown upon his desk. 'We still have a little time before us,' he said. 'Shall we apply this method to Mr Boost's bale?'

'Rather, Daddy!' exclaimed April. 'Fire away! This is a branch of mathematics which has never occurred to me before. Makes me wish I had been better at sums at school.'

His audience settled themselves more comfortably into their chairs, and the Professor proceeded.

CHAPTER XIII

'VERY well, then,' said the Professor, settling himself down once more to the didactic style. 'Let us proceed to a consideration of the circumstances surrounding this bale of Mr Boost, of which, as Denbigh points out, we have only hearsay evidence.

'It is stated that a bale, said to contain the case of a grand-father clock and certain other articles, none of which were of any obvious value, and none of which were of a nature to tempt an ordinary thief, was collected on the afternoon of the day with which we are concerned, and delivered to Mr Boost's address. The people concerned in this transaction, so far as we know, are, a man called Samuels and his nephew, a carter whom we know as George, and Mr Boost himself. Of George we know nothing beyond his Christian name, and the fact that he had performed similar services for Mr Boost on other occasions. Mr Boost is known to us as Harold's landlord, as the proprietor of a second-hand furniture business, and as an avowed Communist. In the latter capacity he has a distinct aversion for the police. This point is of interest in connection with the disappearance of the bale, for it is extremely unlikely that he would report its loss to the authorities, a factor which may well have been taken into account by the thief, if we admit the truth of Mr Boost's statement.'

'As a matter of fact, I suggested that he should communicate with the police as soon as he told me about it,' put in Harold. 'As you say, sir, he scoffed at the idea.'

'Exactly,' assented the Professor. 'Now, Inspector Hanslet told me something of this man Boost. He is what I may term an idealistic Communist, one who thoroughly believes in the holiness of his cause, and allows no consideration of personal gain to vitiate it. In Inspector Hanslet's own words, he is considered

114

"Straight," and is a man whose word may be safely accepted. I, personally, therefore, am inclined to accept his statements as correct, in the absence of any evidence to the contrary.'

'I agree with you there, sir,' said Harold, in response to a glance from the Professor in his direction. 'I've always found him perfectly honest, in spite of his extraordinary theories.'

'Accepting Mr Boost's statements, then, this bale was placed in the porch of Number 16, Riverside Gardens, some time between Harold's departure that evening and his return. We have, I admit, no confirmation of his statement, although we have corroborative evidence of the bale leaving the address in Camberwell from which it was despatched.'

'May I make a suggestion?' said Denbigh, as the Professor paused. 'I am prepared to accept Mr Boost's word, and to admit the validity of this corroborative evidence, since it satisfies you. But even so, Mr Boost never saw the bale, he only had this man George's word that it was delivered. In fact, we really know nothing of the bale from the time it left Camberwell, or wherever it was. What was to prevent its being tampered with or even stolen on the journey, either with or without George's connivance? In order to cover himself, George may have declared that the bale was delivered. He can produce no signature for it.'

'Here, I admit, we have no facts to guide us,' replied the Professor quietly. 'You will remember my warning, that we are only constructing theories which must be submitted to the test of facts. If necessary, I think we can secure the facts we require to confirm George's story. You know the topography of Riverside Gardens. I understand that you have visited Harold there. It is a cul-de-sac, narrow and ill-paved. The arrival of any vehicle capable of transporting such a bale as has been described to us can hardly have failed to cause sufficient stir to attract the attention of some, at least, of its inhabitants. If we find it necessary to confirm George's story, we should have no difficulty in securing the necessary evidence.'

'Oh, yes, let's believe in this bale, it makes the story much more exciting!' exclaimed April. 'I'd just as soon believe George the carter as I would George Washington. Fire away, Daddy.'

Professor Priestley, thus exhorted, continued. 'Now, turning from this man George, let us consider the source from which this bale originated. We are immediately struck by the remarkable similarity between the source and the destination. In each case we have a second-hand furniture business. Nothing could be more likely than that one second-hand dealer should have business transactions with another. Mr Boost was in no way surprised that his colleague should send him such a bale; we may infer from his attitude that such transactions were by no means uncommon. But there is a further point of interest. We are told that Mr Boost's colleague, Samuels by name, was also a communist. But here the resemblance ends. This Samuels, whose real name we believe to be Szamuelly, was a communist of quite a different type from Mr Boost.

'You may remember the six months' Bolshevist ascendancy in Hungary under the régime of Bela Kun, in which a man of the name of Szamuelly played a notorious part, and finally committed suicide in order to avoid capture. Mr Boost believes this man to be a connection of Samuels, the second-hand dealer. Now the Communists of Bela Kun were anything but idealists. They were merely brigands whose object it was to snatch advantage for themselves out of the general state of disorder produced by their régime. Samuels is undoubtedly a man of this type. He seems, according to Mr Boost, to be suspected of betraying his comrades, and to bear an evil reputation in consequence. In fact, I dare say we should not be far wrong in assuming him to be a man who has amassed a certain sum of money by playing a double game, by insinuating himself into favour with various parties, and acting treacherously towards them in turn. You will admit that such an assumption is permissible, Denbigh?'

Denbigh, thus suddenly appealed to, moved restlessly on the sofa. 'Really, Professor, I can hardly say,' he replied. 'I can see no reason to doubt it; such men do exist, I suppose. I expect the police know all about him.'

'Undoubtedly they do,' agreed the Professor. 'Inspector Hanslet will perhaps be able to supply us with facts in this direction, should we decide to apply to him. But for the present let us form a mental picture of this man. Again, we have only hearsay evidence about him; so far as we know, none of us have ever seen him. According to the description of Mr Boost and others, he is an old man, of irritable temperament, suffering apparently from some bronchial affection which produces difficulty in breathing, and of remarkably slovenly appearance. His hair is always untended and is allowed to grow as it pleases, he is never known to have shaved, and his clothes appear to have been selected at random from the unsaleable stock of his shop. His only acknowledged relative is a nephew who occasionally assists him in his business. Harold has actually seen that nephew, whose name is said to be Isidore. Can you describe him, Harold?'

'No, sir, I can't say that I can,' replied Harold. 'I only saw him for a minute or two, and the shop was almost completely dark at the time. He seemed to be of medium height, and he stooped and shuffled as he walked. He talked in a husky sort of a whisper, and rambled as though he were half daft. From what I could see of his face, I got the impression that he had a tendency towards the same shagginess as his uncle. I fancy I should know him again if I saw him.'

'Would you, I wonder?' said the Professor, reflectively. 'Recognition of a man only seen in the circumstances you describe is usually very difficult. The light of day often produces an entirely different impression. However, that is immaterial. You saw this nephew Isidore some days after the disappearance of the bale from the porch of Mr Boost's shop. He informed you, I understand, that he packed the bale according to his uncle's instructions, and delivered it personally to George the carter. That is correct, is it not?'

'Quite, sir,' replied Harold. 'As soon as I learnt that, which was what I had come to find out, I left the place. I'm afraid I didn't take any more notice of the fellow.'

'Naturally,' said the Professor. 'You had, in fact, done all that was expected of you. You did not see the uncle on this occasion, I understand?'

'No, sir, he was ill in bed,' replied Harold. 'He was in a room which led off the shop. I could hear him wheezing and coughing and grumbling at his nephew before Isidore came into the shop in reply to my knocking. I must say he sounded a remarkably unpleasant old man.'

'No doubt, no doubt,' agreed the Professor. 'Even Mr Boost appears to have been reluctant to brave his tongue. Now, as to this difficulty in breathing which you describe. I imagine that such a condition is typical of a certain type of disorder, is it not, Denbigh?'

'Most certainly,' replied Denbigh readily. 'An asthmatic affection of almost any kind would produce the symptoms Merefield describes. If it is correct that he was having an altercation with his nephew, the effort involved would account for a considerable degree of such wheezing and coughing. I daresay that if he kept quiet, he would find considerable relief. For instance, while his nephew was with you and he was left alone, I expect that the symptoms abated?'

'As a matter of fact, I don't remember hearing him then,' said Harold. 'It may have been that I wasn't listening, though.'

'Ah! My diagnosis is correct,' replied Denbigh in a tone of satisfaction. 'I think we may safely add to our list the fact that Mr Samuels suffers from asthma, if that is of any use.'

'All facts are of value, whether we recognise that value or not,' said the Professor, gravely. 'But to proceed. We are faced with a difficulty which it must be our business to solve. According to the statement of Isidore Samuels, a bale left Inkerman Street, Camberwell, containing the case of a grandfather clock and certain other articles. According to the theory

I have already explained to you, a similar bale, purporting to be the same, but containing an unidentified corpse, was unpacked some hours later by the second man concerned in the entry to Harold's rooms.

'Now there are two theories which may be advanced to account for this difficulty. In the first place, two bales may have existed, one containing a grandfather clock, the second a human body. The description of the bale given by George the carter may apply to either or both, the weight and the dimensions in each case would be approximately the same, taking into consideration the statement that with the clock case were packed a number of solid statuettes. In this case the body bale must have been substituted for the clock bale either at some point during the journey between Camberwell and Riverside Gardens, or after its delivery at the latter address. In the second place, one bale only existed. In that case, either my theory falls to the ground, and we have to account for the disappearance of a bale containing a clock case and some statuettes from the porch of Mr Boost's shop some time in the evening, or the bale collected by George from Inkerman Street actually contained, not a clock, but a body.'

'Daddy dear, your logic is unassailable!' interrupted April. 'But surely the Samuels family could find a simpler method of disposing of the bodies of their victims than dumping them on Harold's bed for all the world to see? Think of the danger of the corpse being recognised!'

'Not so fast, my dear,' replied the Professor indulgently. 'Let us examine these theories in turn. I confess that the probability of two bales having existed does not appear to me to be very great. You will allow that if the exchange was effected *before* the delivery to Riverside Gardens, it would hardly have been without the connivance of George. Now, again according to Mr Boost, it was George himself who first drew Mr Boost's attention to the existence of the bale. But for George, it might have been some considerable time before he became aware of it. If

George were implicated, it seems unlikely that he would deliberately call attention to the matter. If, on the other hand, the exchange was made *after* the delivery of the bale, whoever made it must have incurred considerable risk of detection. The same remarks that I made as to the stir caused by the arrival of the first bale apply with equal force to that of the second. Again, why should the first bale have been removed or in any way interfered with? The theory of the existence of more than one bale offers, on the whole, more difficulties than it would appear to solve.

'I am, therefore, inclined to turn my attention to the probability of only one bale being involved in the matter. In that case, if my theory that the bale contained the body found by Harold is correct, it must have contained it when it left Inkerman Street. In other words, the body originated in or passed through Samuels' shop.'

'Then old Samuels must have been the murderer!' exclaimed Harold. 'I shouldn't be surprised, from all I've heard of him. Besides, that would explain his sudden departure. But I wonder who the fellow was that was killed!'

'You and April are alike in jumping too quickly to conclusions,' said the Professor with a smile. 'In the first place, the verdict of the inquest tells us that there was no murder, that the old man, whoever he was, died a natural death. In the absence of any evidence to the contrary, we are bound to accept that conclusion. In the second place, why should Samuels be any more likely to be guilty than his nephew? If it is correct, as you say, that the old man was bedridden, it is not beyond the bounds of possibility that Isidore disposed of the body by this means without his uncle's knowledge. But remember that we have no evidence, merely a suspicion that one of these two knew of the existence of the body.

'With that warning, consider the matter from a new angle. One of the Samuels has a body to dispose of, no matter for the moment under what circumstances. Suppose, if you like, that one of their associates died at Inkerman Street. The Samuels family, in common with Mr Boost, have an understandable reluctance to calling the attention of the authorities to their affairs. It occurs to them to wrap the body up in a bale of sacking, with no doubt a suitable stiffening to disguise the nature of the package, and to dispatch it to Mr Boost's address, knowing that individual to be away. I imagine that to have been the form in which the idea first occurred to the man who carried it out. The perfecting of the idea may have come later. One of the Samuels recollected that he had means of access to Mr Boost's house. We can believe that, at one time, a certain intimacy existed between the comrades, and possibly Samuels possessed a key. If this were the case, everything becomes clear. Either Samuels or his nephew was the second man concerned in entering Harold's room that night.'

'It must have been young Isidore, then!' exclaimed Harold excitedly. 'I thought he wasn't such a fool as he looked when I heard how neatly he had disappeared the other afternoon! It can't have been the old man, he wouldn't have had the strength to carry the body upstairs. Why on earth didn't I think of all this when I saw him?'

'You would have had no evidence,' replied the Professor. Then he turned towards Denbigh, half apologetically. 'You will realise that so far I am only propounding theories,' he said. 'There is no evidence against Isidore Samuels, either that he was responsible for the death of the man or the disposal of the body. But I think you will agree that the laws of probability point to his being in some way involved.'

'Perhaps so,' replied Denbigh, quietly. 'But surely, Professor, the best way of ascertaining the truth of the matter is to put the police on his track?'

'On what charge?' retorted the Professor, swiftly. 'Murder? The man died a natural death, we are told, and I doubt whether exhumation and a second examination would result in any other verdict. Housebreaking? I fancy Inspector Hanslet would want more tangible evidence before issuing a warrant upon such a charge. No, there may be a method of dealing with Isidore Samuels, but that is not it. Besides, I understand that he has disappeared. For the present, at all events, I should prefer to act somewhat differently. Remember, the main object of my investigation into this matter is to restore Harold to his former position, to clear him of any complicity in the matter. Indeed, so indifferent am I to the technical morality of the case, that, were I in a position to confront this nephew and obtain an account of his actions, I should be fully satisfied, without any resource to the authorities.'

'Isn't that what's called being an accessory after the fact?' enquired April. 'Upon my word, Daddy, I didn't think it of you! Now go on, there's a dear, and deduce for us who the man was that Harold found.'

'My dear, when you reach my age you will realise that the attraction of a problem lies purely in its solution, and not in any consequences which that solution may have. But you mention a very interesting point—the identity of the dead man. Let us consider it for a moment. We have, then, a corpse, which, before the verdict of the coroner's jury, the police were very anxious to identify. Inspector Hanslet has informed me of the methods which they have at their disposal. In addition to these methods, a description and photograph of the dead man was published in the Press and at every police station. Yet nobody came forward who could identify him. There were, of course, the usual number of applicants to see the corpse, some impelled, no doubt, by curiosity, others by the fear or hope of recognising a missing relative or friend. But none of them could name the man they saw.

'Now, under the present system of civilisation, it is almost inconceivable that anyone could live so solitary a life that his complete disappearance should attract no attention, and the active advertisement of his characteristics should be unrecognised. For my own part, I am forced to conclude either that the deceased was known only to a limited circle, every member of which was interested in maintaining silence, or that his appearance in death was totally different from that which he presented in life, in other words, that when alive he wore a disguise, natural or artificial.'

'By Jove, some Communist fellow who wanted to hide his identity!' exclaimed Harold.

'I am also of the opinion,' continued the Professor, disregarding the interruption, 'that the corpse was disguised, if I may use the expression. Not, of course, in essentials, for that is obviously impossible, but in just those respects by which men are commonly known from one another. I have already explained my theory that the second man changed clothes with the corpse. You will remember that the dead man's clothes and boots were tightly fitting, that he seemed to possess no hat or overcoat. I think it quite possible that the second man decamped in the clothes which belonged to the dead man. These may have been thoroughly characteristic; did we know the nature of them, we should quite likely have abundant clues to the dead man's identity. As it is, the clothes found on the body were carefully chosen to afford no clues whatever. I attach no importance to the trifles found in the pockets. As I have already stated, they seem to me to have been put there with the express purpose of creating a wrong impression.

'Now, why should not the man who prepared these clothes have gone a step further? If, indeed, he were Isidore Samuels, and he contrived that the body should be conveyed by the innocent George to Riverside Gardens, it is almost certain that the man died at Inkerman Street, according to medical evidence, not later than that morning. George called about four o'clock, a fact which I ask you to bear in mind. Isidore had, therefore, the corpse in his possession some time before its removal, more than enough for him to pack it in the bale. We have seen that he was anxious to hide its identity. Why should he not have taken the most effective means possible to this end?'

'Surely you can't make up a dead body, Daddy?' enquired April.

'Not by any means which would escape detection,' replied the Professor. 'But you can carry out the reverse process. Now what was the description of the body circulated by the police? Indeed, you saw the body yourself, Harold. How would you describe it?'

'Oh, yes, I saw quite enough of it,' replied Harold feelingly. 'Inspector Hanslet seemed determined that I should recognise it. It was that of an elderly man, clean shaven, hair recently cut—the experts said it was dyed in some way. Whoever it was, had obviously been very particular about his personal appearance.'

'Exactly,' said the Professor in a satisfied tone. 'You, as everybody else, having seen the clothes and boots the man was wearing, were only too ready to see the corroborative evidence of the man's care for his appearance. But I would ask you to answer this question. What if this care for his appearance began after his death?'

'Why, what on earth do you mean, sir?' exclaimed Harold.

'It seems clear enough,' replied the Professor. 'What if all this shaving, this cutting and dyeing of the hair, was a device of Isidore Samuels' to screen the identity of the corpse; if, between the man's death and his removal from Inkerman Street, he had been so treated? Inspector Hanslet and everybody else connected with the case was so convinced that the man died in your rooms that such a possibility never occurred to them. Now you begin to appreciate fully the reasons for all those false tracks so carefully laid, and the ingenuity which underlay the whole drama. The man did not die at Riverside Gardens, but at Inkerman Street. Further, in life, he was probably the very antithesis of the body as found by you. I imagine him hirsute, slovenly, utterly careless of his appearance. Now then, I ask you, can you form any opinion as to his identity?'

'Why, you can't mean old Samuels, sir!' replied Harold in a

puzzled tone. 'I heard him, about a week after the body was found, and at least two people saw him get into a four-wheeler and drive to Waterloo Station.'

'Ah, yes, that brings us to the question of the disappearance of both Samuels and his nephew,' replied the Professor. He was about to continue, when the study door opened and Mary entered.

'There's a lady to see you, sir,' she said. 'She gave no name, but said that you were expecting her.'

'Ah, yes. Thank you, Mary. That is quite right,' replied the Professor. 'Please do not disturb yourselves. I will return very shortly.'

He rose and left the room. His audience, silent under the surprise of the unusual interruption, could hear the sound of voices in the hall without. In less than a minute the door opened once more, and Professor Priestley appeared, his hand upon the arm of a woman, whose face and form were indistinguishable in the dim light.

CHAPTER XIV

THE fire had fallen low in the grate, and it was impossible for those in the study to see more than the outline of the figure which accompanied Professor Priestley into the room. There was a general movement, as they rose from their chairs, but the Professor's voice, sharp and authoritative, checked any words before they were spoken.

'Please sit down!' he exclaimed, and Harold heard again the note of sternness which had impressed itself upon him on that memorable day when they had discussed *Aspasia*. 'This lady has kindly consented to attend our discussion. It is possible that she may be able to throw light upon certain phases of the matter which at present are obscure. Will you be good enough to take this chair?'

As the Professor led his guest to a seat in the corner of the room, remote from the glow of the fire or the reflection of the light cast upon his desk, Harold felt a dull wave of despair sweep through him. All had been going so well. He had complete faith in the Professor's theory of the events of the fatal night; as each point was developed with relentless logic, he felt the burden of suspicion which had weighed him down lighten and vanish as a mist before the sun. His seat was close to April's, he could hear the gladness in her voice as his innocence was made clear, knew for himself that she, too, rejoiced at the lifting of the cloud. And now, when all was clear, when the guilt was shifted from his shoulders to those of a remote stranger, the one person in the world who could blacken him in her eyes had descended between them like the dark mantle of fate.

For he could have no doubt that this was Vere. What her mission was he could guess only too well. She alone could tell of her dealings with Isidore Samuels, could provide the motive for the death of the old man, could clinch the matter to the satisfaction of all concerned. A valuable witness, certainly, from the Professor's point of view. But, in the process, how could she fail to recount the whole story of her relations with himself? He checked a fervent desire to dash from the room, to escape from the ordeal of hearing the intimate details of his life revealed before April. He sank back into his chair, the victim of utter hopelessness. For a moment he had dreamed that even now it might not be too late, that perhaps April could forgive the past, even that the old friendship between them might ripen into love. But in the face of the evidence that Vere must give, what choice could April make between his degraded self and the favoured Denbigh?

The woman took her seat in silence; the Professor made his way to his desk, and continued his discourse as though there had been no interruption.

'I come now to the evening, only a few days ago, when Harold and Mr Boost went to Camberwell to visit Mr Samuels' shop,' he began. 'For the benefit of those of you who do not know what occurred on that occasion, I will explain that they found the place on fire. I have ascertained since that it was completely destroyed. On questioning various residents in the neighbourhood, they received two pieces of information, both of which are of considerable interest. The first of these was that Mr Samuels, or someone greatly resembling him, had been seen to enter a cab, of which the driver was instructed to drive to Waterloo Station. The second was that, some time later, Isidore Samuels made his way out of the burning house.

'Now, at first sight, this appears to dispose of the theory that the body found by Harold was that of Mr Samuels. A man who has been dead nearly a fortnight, and buried under the supervision of the authorities, cannot, in our experience, leave a house by his own volition and enter a cab. But, I would ask you, what evidence have we that the man who entered the cab was indeed Mr Samuels?'

There was no reply to the Professor's rhetorical question. In the pause that ensued the only sound was that of the rapid breathing of his audience. The Professor, in a firm voice, continued:

'The evidence is that of two neighbours, who, at first sight, seem not likely to have been mistaken. Mr Samuels was familiar to them; they were acquainted with his characteristic asthmatic symptoms, with his general appearance. At a distance, say, of thirty or forty paces they recognised him by these very signs. But put yourselves in an analogous position. You know, for example, the tenant of a given house. During the period in which you have been his neighbours, you have noticed his peculiarities, the various points which distinguish him in your minds from his fellow-beings. One day, a man, conforming in these respects to your ideas of your neighbour, comes out of the door of his house, enters a cab, calls out an instruction to the driver, and goes away. Such an event causes you no surprise, and very little interest. There is nothing in the incident arousing your critical powers. The event registers itself automatically upon your memory and, if questioned subsequently, you would declare that your neighbour had gone away in a cab; you knew it because you had seen and heard him.

'The case of the eye-witnesses in Inkerman Street is exactly similar. They believed Mr Samuels was alone in his house, possibly from previous experience that he was in the habit of leaving in a cab. They naturally inferred that any man leaving the house must be Mr Samuels, an inference supported by the corroboration of his gait, his appearance, and his asthmatic symptoms. So ready were they to believe that this man was Mr Samuels, that I maintain that anybody sufficiently familiar with him to impersonate his chief characteristics, and to assume a rough disguise simulating his appearance, would have conveyed to them the impression that he was Mr Samuels himself.'

'But, Daddy dear, that doesn't account for the conversation overheard by Harold the first time he went into the shop to see

Mr Samuels,' objected April. And at the sound of her voice a faint movement could be heard from the corner where the strange woman sat.

'If we allow that the impersonator of Mr Samuels in the incident of the cab could reproduce his voice sufficiently well to deceive the neighbours, who knew him, we can assume that he could do so easily enough to satisfy Harold, who had never heard him,' rejoined the Professor. 'My theory of the sequence of events on Harold's first visit to Inkerman Street is this. When he first knocked at the door of Mr Samuels' shop, the place was empty. Isidore Samuels arrived later, possibly by the back entrance, which we are informed existed in Balaclava Street. Indeed, Harold actually saw a man enter the passage leading to that entrance, who may or may not have been Isidore himself. At all events, when Harold knocked the second time, the nephew heard him, and from the back room began his imitation of his uncle's speech and symptoms. Remember, again, that everything happened as Harold expected. He believed that Mr Samuels was in the house, and was therefore prepared to accept any, even the slightest, evidence of his presence without question. It is only when something happens which we do not expect that we begin to inquire into circumstances, that our suspicions are aroused, in fact.

'Now, this is shortly my belief of what has occurred during the past fortnight. Mr Samuels died on the afternoon prior to Harold finding the body on his bed. This is in accordance with the medical evidence. This death was accurately forecasted by his nephew, for he had *previously* instructed George to collect the bale. Alternatively, for I am anxious to cast no unnecessary suspicion upon Isidore in the absence of confirmatory evidence, it had really been decided to send a clock-case to Mr Boost, and the body was only substituted at the last moment.

'For some reason Isidore was anxious not to proclaim the fact of his uncle's death. He was faced, therefore, with a double problem, the disposal of the body, and the accounting for the disappearance of Mr Samuels. This problem he solved in what, I am bound to admit, was a highly ingenious manner. I have already explained how he disposed of the body, after rendering it unidentifiable by anybody but himself, the only person, as far as we know, who knew his uncle really intimately. Once more, remember that at this time nobody but himself knew that Mr Samuels was dead. If they had, they might have searched more closely for marks which might identify the unknown body with Mr Samuels.'

Again the Professor paused, and a silence prevailed in the study. It seemed that the atmosphere was becoming tense, that forces were being brought into play which must eventually result in some strange outbreak. And as the Professor continued, a faint sigh, as of relief, fluttered into the stillness.

'The essential thing, if all suspicion was to be avoided, was that Mr Samuels' disappearance should not be connected with the discovery of the body. Isidore ensured this by maintaining the fiction of Mr Samuels' presence at Inkerman Street for a full ten days after the body was found. If any enquiries were subsequently made, they would date from the time when Mr Samuels was last seen alive, that is to say, from the time that the supposed Mr Samuels was seen to drive away in a cab.

'That it was actually Isidore who entered that cab I have no doubt. He had plenty of time to reach Waterloo Station, leave it again by some other exit, change his disguise, and return to Inkerman Street. His task was still unfinished. It was not safe for him to remain at Inkerman Street indefinitely; sooner or later enquiries were bound to be made for his uncle. Nor was it safe to abandon the place and leave it empty. Far better to destroy it, and with it every clue which could lead to the detection of his actions. He set fire to the house, remained until he was sure that it was well alight, and then vanished in a way which once more proved his resourcefulness. His escape in the stolen clothes through a crowd whose attention was riveted upon something else is a masterpiece, if only in its simplicity.

He has only to avoid the neighbourhood of Camberwell, the society of his acquaintances there, and his safety is virtually assured.'

'But what is the object of all this, Daddy?' put in April. 'Why hide the death of his uncle in this elaborate way?'

'It is possible to imagine many reasons,' replied the Professor gravely. 'Perhaps he wished to secure his uncle's money, which is said to have been kept in the shop. Perhaps, even, he was not altogether guiltless of his death. In the absence of any facts bearing upon these points we cannot say. But there is one very curious aspect of the matter, which I have not yet touched upon. That is the victimisation of Harold.

'You will remember that my theory of the disposal of the body assumes that the nephew had access to Harold's rooms, presumably by means of the possession of keys of the front door and the door of Harold's sitting room. This may or may not have been fortuitous. Either Isidore Samuels, remembering that such keys were available, decided to use Harold's rooms as a depository for his uncle's body, or for some reason he had decided previously that these rooms were the most suitable place in London for such deposition, and had taken steps to secure the means of entrance to them. I think, on the whole, that there has been a subsequent attempt to saddle Harold with complicity in the matter. I refer, of course, to the remarkable article which appeared in *The Weekly Record*, and with which we are all familiar.

'Now, this article is one of the most peculiar factors in the case. It was brilliantly written, and it revealed an extraordinary knowledge of Harold's life. In addition to this, it was obviously framed with the object of concentrating upon Harold the search for the motive for the presence of the body in his rooms. Now, it might be argued that Isidore had a reason for drawing attention to Harold, since attention directed upon Harold would be diverted from himself, and for that reason inspired the article. But there appear to me to be two or three circumstances which would seem to render these reasons insufficient. In the first place, I should have thought that Isidore ran more risk by associating himself with the matter than he would have acquired gain by its appearance. In the second place, the circumstances attending the reception of the article are peculiar. I must explain that I obtained an introduction to the editor of *The Weekly Record* through Lord Sevenoaks, its proprietor. From him I learnt that the article in question was sent by post, typewritten in the ordinary way, with a brief note written on the paper of the Hotel Gigantic, and signed with the name Ralph Tomlinson. It appears that a gentleman of that name is an occasional contributor to *The Weekly Record* of articles of a similar nature. The editor accepted the article in good faith, and was considerably astonished when he was informed later that Ralph Tomlinson had left England some months ago. On enquiry at the Hotel Gigantic, he was informed that there was no record of any person of that name having stayed there.

'Now I think you will agree that this points to the writer being inspired with a desire to have the article printed, and at the same time to conceal his own identity. It is easy enough for anyone to acquire hotel note-paper; he has only to walk into the writing-room and take it. Whoever wrote the article guessed that the name of a contributor would incline the editor to publish it. A newspaper office was hardly likely to compare the handwriting of the note with that of previous communications from the real Ralph Tomlinson. Finally, if by any means his fraud were discovered, it would be practically impossible to trace the sender of the letter. On the whole, I am very much inclined to suspect Isidore Samuels of being the author of that article.'

'But surely, Daddy dear, that seems hardly likely,' said April. 'You said yourself that it was very well written and well reasoned, you know you did at the time. I can hardly believe that the nephew of old Samuels, a second-hand dealer in the slums, would be capable of writing such a thing.'

'Ah!' replied the Professor gravely. 'That leads us to a closer examination of the true identity of Isidore Samuels. You will remember that, according to the evidence we have obtained, Isidore was absent from his uncle's shop all day, and only appeared there at intervals, usually in the evenings. Now, we do not know the exact nature of Mr Samuels' true business, for which I fancy the second-hand furniture trade was little more than a mask. But, whatever it was, it did not involve any considerable number of customers visiting his shop. The fact that the latter was closed all day for some time, on the plea of Mr Samuels' illness, does not appear to have occasioned any surprise or inconvenience in the neighbourhood.

'Again, the shop had a back entrance in Balaclava Street, a point that we must bear in mind. I think that it is highly probable that Isidore Samuels made use of this back entrance for his comings and goings to his uncle's shop, and that, although it was generally assumed that he spent the night there, he only visited it for a short time in the evening, probably to avert any suspicion which might be caused by its remaining continually locked up. If this were the case, Isidore Samuels had the remainder of the twenty-four hours at his disposal, in which to assume an altogether different rôle from that of the nephew of Mr Samuels.

'As to what that rôle may have been, we can only speculate. But the theory throws a new light upon his actions on the evening of the fire. He was anxious, now that his uncle's body had been safely disposed of, and he had had time to reap whatever advantage he could expect from his death, to destroy completely all traces of the past. From that moment he could assume for good the second rôle which he had been intermittently playing already, and cut himself entirely free from all association with Samuels and Inkerman Street. No doubt it is in this rôle that he exists now, and, should we desire to trace the author of the whole of the mystery, we should be compelled to search for an individual as unlike Isidore Samuels as our imagination would allow. Remember, he changed the appearance of his uncle's body in such a way that it seemed at first sight absurd that it should be that of Mr Samuels. We may be sure that he is more than capable of changing his own appearance, a very much easier task, so that very few even of those with whom he was intimate would recognise him.'

'Then it seems pretty hopeless,' suggested April. 'After all, why should we worry? Harold is cleared, and that is the only thing that matters.'

'My dear, although Harold may be cleared in our own eyes, we can scarcely expect others to concur in our opinion, unless we can produce facts,' replied the Professor. 'Although, I confess, were I confronted with the man, I should be content with hearing his own account of the matter. My interest in the case is more logical than judicial, I fear.'

He paused for a moment as though collecting his thoughts, and then proceeded:

'Now, what have we to guide us toward the present identity of this Isidore Samuels? Not much, I fear. We have seen him to be a man of considerable resource, as revealed by the ingenuity he displayed at every turn, and of considerable education, as revealed by the article in *The Weekly Record*, if we allow that he was the author. But, apart from this, and to my mind of far greater importance, is the fact that he was acquainted with certain incidents in Harold's life, and had, I believe, an interest in blackening his character, over and above the interest of diverting attention from his own participation in the matter. The author of the article in *The Weekly Record* knew every detail of the crime as it appeared to have been committed, and, in addition, he knew certain facts of Harold's life. He contrived to weave the two into a web of falsehood extremely difficult to disentangle. I refuse to believe that this could have been done by anybody to whom Harold was personally unacquainted.

'Now, I have evidence that, although Harold was unaware of the existence of Isidore Samuels, Isidore was aware of Harold's.

Into that evidence I do not propose to enter; it is immaterial at the moment. It was not in his capacity as Isidore Samuels that the unknown was interested in Harold, but in his second, unknown capacity. For some reason, which can only be guessed at, it was in his interest to blacken Harold's character, to exhibit him in exactly the same light as the author of the article endeavoured to do.'

'But what a rotten shame, Daddy!' burst out April. 'What was his object? The man must be a howling cad, whoever he is.'

'I agree with you entirely, my dear,' replied the Professor. 'A howling cad, perhaps, even something worse. Old Samuels *may* have died a natural death, but, if so, it was remarkably well-timed from his nephew's point of view. Remember, he had already telephoned for George, the carter, to come and remove his body. And further, if he were ever to be traced, question would be sure to arise concerning the cash-box which Mr Samuels is alleged to have kept in his house. Did that perish in the fire? Knowing Isidore's resource, as we have reason to know it, I very much doubt it. No, were he to fall into the hands of the police, I am afraid that he would find it very difficult to extricate himself.

'But to return to the question of the identification of this man in his present guise. I have put before you the general characteristics by which he may be narrowed down to a comparatively small circle, that of Harold's acquaintances. But I have been informed that there is a further distinguishing mark, a most unusual one, by which this individual might be distinguished from his fellow men.'

The Professor leant back in his chair and fixed his gaze upon the lamp standing on his desk. The tension in the room was very near breaking point. Since the entry of the unknown woman neither Harold nor Denbigh had spoken; each had sat motionless, listening in silence to the Professor's inexorable logic, hypnotised by his development of the drama. For a moment

the stillness was profound, and then April, with a restless movement of impatience, broke the spell.

'What is this distinguishing mark, Daddy?' she enquired.

'Isidore Samuels had a birthmark in the form of a cross upon
his left shoulder,' replied the Professor, slowly and distinctly.

'A birthmark in the form of a cross!' repeated April. 'Why,
what an extraordinary thing! When I was bandaging Evan's
arm just now . . .'

But her sentence was never finished. With a sudden movement Professor Priestley tilted the shade of his lamp, until its
rays shone full upon the face of Evan Denbigh, white, staring,
huddled in the corner of the sofa. All leapt to their feet, knowing
somehow that the crisis was imminent, searching for the direction from which it must fall. Then suddenly, as if her immobility
had given place to the speed of a tempest, the unknown woman
leapt across the room, and stood for an instant staring into
Denbigh's eyes.

'Isidore!' she exclaimed. 'So I've found you at last, have I?'

CHAPTER XV

HAROLD, who was nearest the door, sprang for the switches, and plunged the study into a flood of light, as though in this way he could dispel the darkness of utter amazement which possessed him. Vere—Isidore Samuels—Evan Denbigh—three personalities resolved into two—the problem was at first too much for him. And yet, as he stared, fascinated, the white drawn face of Denbigh began to suggest the vaguely remembered outline of the half-daft Isidore, of that hurrying form which had brushed past him to disappear into the gloomy entrance off Balaclava Street. Was it a true resemblance, or was his fancy, exerted by the extraordinary theories of the Professor, playing tricks with him?

April, very white and still, sat with her hands clenched, gazing, not at the man she had known, and this strange woman who confronted him, but into the glowing heart of the fire, as though she could watch there in procession a thousand incidents of her acquaintanceship with Denbigh. A sort of numb horror filled her, an uneasy feeling that the well-ordered safe old world of which she had been a gay ornament, had somehow been arrested suddenly in its course, shooting her far out into a chilly and unknown void, where, as yet, there was nothing for her to cling to. Was it possible she had made a fool of herself?

So that it was left to Denbigh to break the silence, to answer Vere's question, which still seemed to ring shrilly through the room. And his answer was a laugh, low and mirthless, which caused April to shudder and Harold to gasp audibly, so vividly did it recall the queer scene in the dark recess of Mr Samuels' shop.

'You've won, Professor,' he said. 'It serves me right. I never took your brain into consideration. I confess I should like to know what you mean to do about it?'

'That depends very largely upon your own actions,' replied the Professor gravely. 'You will admit that as I unfolded my theory I gave you every chance to confess without the indignity of this exposure. I think it rests with those you have deluded to decide upon the next step.'

Denbigh looked slowly round the room. Harold stood by the door, staring at him as though he were a visitor from another world. Vere, with unfathomable eyes, leant upon the desk, breathing heavily, glancing alternately at him and at the bowed figure of April. The Professor, the tips of his fingers together, had swung round in his chair and sat as a judge awaiting the verdict of a jury.

Slowly, as he struggled to regain his composure, Denbigh's eyes lost their hunted expression, and became hard and bright. There was just a chance, a fighting chance, left. His ambitious scheme had failed, the rôle of Evan Denbigh, the brilliant young scientist, the favoured suitor of April, was no longer possible. But, if he could extricate himself, he could shed the worn disguise, and create some other form in which to enjoy the tangible advantages he had gained. Clearly, with a keen insight into the psychology of these people who unmasked him, he saw the way.

'Your theories withstand the test of fact, Professor,' he said quietly. 'You have reconstructed my actions to the last detail. I am Isidore Samuels, and the body found by Merefield in his rooms was my uncle's. I am responsible for his death, but I believe that morally I should be esteemed as a public benefactor for ridding the world of one of the meanest and most treacherous rascals that ever encumbered it.

'I need not tell you the full story of the man's treachery. I have no doubt that if you ask Mr Boost he can tell you pretty well as much as I know, and perhaps more. Among his other occupations he was a moneylender on a small scale, lending at exorbitant interest to the struggling poor, and once in his clutches there was no escape. One way and another he was responsible for more misery than it seems possible any one man could produce.

'However, as far as I am concerned, all that is only of casual interest. I hated him on far more personal grounds. He drove my mother to prostitution, and then, before I was born, did his best to starve her, and ultimately succeeded. He flung me out of his house when I was a few days old, hoping that I should vanish from his sight for good. For many years I did vanish; starved, ill-treated, my life made a burden to me. But I managed to survive, and when I learnt the story, purely by chance, I determined to have my revenge.

'How I managed to educate myself and become the Evan Denbigh that you knew, hardly matters. I know what it cost me, but I could hardly make you understand that. My uncle never knew anything of that side of my existence. To him I was an idiot nephew who managed to pick up a living somehow, and could be made occasional use of in the shop. Vere, who . . . who has known me for some time, can confirm this if she cares to.'

Vere, thus appealed to, nodded her head. 'Yes, that's right,' she said dully. 'You managed to beg your way along, somehow.'

'I had to beg my way,' replied Isidore quietly. 'I never knew who my father was, but I had blood in my veins which revolted at the name of Samuels, my mother's, and all it implied. Even when I was a child, without a crust to gnaw in the evening, I felt that I could do something if only I had the money. So I begged and starved and spent every penny on being taught. The only thing that kept me going was the realisation that science, which seemed so hard to acquire to young men with every advantage which I lacked, came to me almost without effort.

'However, I need not bore you with all that. As you know, I eventually gained for myself a position as Sir Alured Faversham's assistant. And there, suddenly, some six months ago, the idea came to me.

'You must know that Sir Alured's chief occupation is the synthetic production of drugs designed to cure various illnesses. It is his life's work, and he has, as you know, been extremely successful. Latterly he has been engaged upon the isolation of a compound which should have a beneficial effect upon asthmatic and bronchial symptoms. It was while I was assisting him with this, that I began to see my way clear before me.

'As you know, Professor, the difficulty with a new and unknown preparation does not end with its adaption to the cure of certain symptoms. It often happens that the drug which will cure the diseases of one organ cannot be made use of, because it produces an ill-effect upon some other organ. From our knowledge of the substances with which we were working, it appeared to us that one of the drugs we succeeded in isolating, which has a very long name, but which we will call the new drug, though it would have a very beneficial effect upon asthmatic cases, would be exceedingly dangerous to employ in adequate doses, since it belonged to that class of compounds which have an ill-effect upon the heart. Whether it would be possible to employ it could only be decided in one way, by experiment. And I decided to make that experiment.

'Isaac Samuels, as I knew from my own observation, suffered from what is properly known as a weak heart. He might have lived for years, or he might have died at very short notice. He also suffered from a form of chronic asthma, the very type of complaint which the new drug was designed to cure. Here was an ideal subject for my experiment. If he died, he had no relatives but myself, and his death would be a positive benefit to the community. If he lived and was cured of his asthma, the safety of the new drug would have been vindicated, and I should have shared in the advantage of its discovery.'

The Professor, who had been listening intently, exclaimed with annoyance, 'I recollect that Faversham told me some time ago that he was on the track of a new drug to alleviate asthma,' he said. 'A fact which I had overlooked and failed to place in its correct sequence! But I shall be glad to hear how you conducted your experiment.'

'My first care was to provide for the event of its failure,' replied Isidore in a level voice. 'Of course, Sir Alured knew nothing of my intentions. If my uncle died, I should be compelled to dispose of his body and to account for his disappearance. There was no risk of the cause of death being revealed by post-mortem. The new drug undergoes chemical changes in the human body and all traces of it vanish within a few hours. Although we had not yet made experiments on human beings, I knew this from our experiments on animals, and from the analogy of similar drugs, already in everyday use. My principal difficulty, therefore, was to dispose of the body, and to deposit it in such a place that no connection could be traced between it and Isidore Samuels or Evan Denbigh.

'I spent a long time considering this problem, and found the solution by accident. I was in the habit of visiting Vere in her rooms, to beg for money, as she has told you, for the method of life which I had adopted required more support than was afforded by the salary I received. One day I noticed that she had lying on her table a pair of Yale keys, which I knew were not those of her rooms, since their lock was of an entirely different pattern. I contrived to pocket them without her notice, and thus gain access to some place, I did not know where, perhaps the office she worked in, which could be used as my depository, if necessary. My plan was already half-formed, and I was only seeking some utterly unlikely spot for my purposes.

'I discovered a little later that Vere was intimate with Merefield, and it immediately occurred to me that these might be the keys of his rooms. I had already cultivated Merefield's acquaintance, in my Denbigh capacity, as I had an idea that access to Mr Boost, whom I knew to be acquainted with my uncle, might some day be useful. I called on Merefield one

evening, with the intention of securing an opportunity of trying
my keys in his locks. Here I met with a stroke of luck. Merefield
was dressing in his bedroom, and his keys were lying on the
table of his sitting-room. I compared his with mine and found
them identical. At the same time I took a good look round the
rooms to get my bearings.'

'Yes, Harold told me of that visit,' said the Professor. 'I think
I see the whole matter clearly now. The traces of hyperdermic
injections on the body, for which I could find no explanation,
are accounted for.'

'You have deduced my actions exactly,' continued Isidore. 'I
began by giving my uncle minute injections of the new drug,
in order to observe its effects. A whiff of anæsthetic while he
was asleep served my purpose and prevented him from having
any knowledge of it. The effect even of those doses was magical,
his asthma practically left him, but I could see that his heart
was adversely affected. It was still doubtful whether he could
stand a large enough dose to effect permanent relief. I determined to make the final experiment on an afternoon when Sir
Alured did not expect me at the laboratory. My arrangements
were soon made; I ensured that Harold should be absent from
his rooms that evening, and I telephoned George, the carter, to
call at Inkerman Street. If my uncle survived, I had a bale,
containing a clock and some statuettes, ready for him.

'I returned early to Inkerman Street that afternoon, and found
my uncle half-asleep in his chair, as I had hoped. A little anæsthetic was sufficient to ensure compliance on his part, and I
injected the dose I had determined upon. It was immediately
apparent that my experiment had failed. His heart grew steadily
weaker, and he died within an hour, without recovering
consciousness or suffering in any way. The rest you know,
Professor, since you have just explained it to us.'

He ceased, and for a moment there was silence. Then
suddenly Vere spoke, hoarsely, but with uncontrollable interest.
'What did you do with the old man's money?' she exclaimed.

Isidore turned to her with a smile. 'Oh, I made sure of that,' he replied. 'I told you that I should have all the money I needed in future.'

The Professor nodded and turned to Harold. 'You hear what this man says,' he said gravely. 'I fancy that, in essentials, at all events, he speaks the truth. With you, as being the living individual most nearly affected by his actions, lies the first word as to what course should be taken. A word on the telephone will bring Inspector Hanslet here, I am sure.'

Before Harold could answer, Vere sprang round the desk to Isidore's side, and stood in front of him, as though to protect him from physical assault.

'You shan't touch him!' she exclaimed. 'He's been a brute to me, I'll allow, and you can say he murdered old Samuels if you like. But if anybody ever deserved murdering, it was that old swine. And now you want to hand Isidore over to the police. Oh, you were all jolly glad to know him when you thought he was doing well. I'll go into the box and tell them everything, how he was encouraged to come here, and what he came for. I'll make you squirm, all of you, let me tell you that. You make me come here on the promise that I can help to clear Harold, and then surprise me into giving Isidore away. Oh, I've been a fool, I know, but I'll make you pay for it if you touch Isidore, you mark my words.'

The Professor held up his hand in a vain attempt to check the torrent of vituperation, but it was not until Vere's breath failed her that she ceased.

'May I ask what is the true relationship between you and this man?' he enquired mildly.

'You might have guessed that long ago!' she replied scornfully. 'He's my husband, and whatever he's done I'm going to stick to him. He did his best for me after all; offered to release me when I had a chance of something better. Oh, yes, he had his own nest to feather, I'll allow. But he won't want to get rid of me for a second time, I warrant.'

She turned suddenly to Isidore and caught him by the arm, dragging him from the sofa on which he was still seated.

"We are going out of this house, and I would like to see who'll stop us,' she continued menacingly. 'And if there's mud to be thrown afterwards, I'll take precious good care to see where most of it sticks. Oh, we'll have the whole story out if you interfere with us, never fear!'

She walked swiftly towards the door, her arm closely linked in Isidore's. Harold made a move as though to intercept them, but April, suddenly awakening from her apparent stupor, stretched out an appealing hand to arrest him.

'Let them go!' she said in a clear voice. 'I couldn't bear it, Daddy! Daddy dear, don't let him stop them!'

Harold, irresolute, turned towards her and Vere and her husband gained the door without opposition. Vere turned for a moment as they passed him. 'Good-bye. Harold,' she whispered, half-regretfully. 'We shan't trouble you again now, never fear.'

The Professor gave no sign, either of assent or dissent. The three left behind in the study heard Vere's eager fingers fumbling with the lock of the front door, heard the door open and slam behind them. Not till then did the Professor speak.

'That is the end I hoped for!' he exclaimed quietly. 'It is not our business to bring this man to justice, even if a jury would convict upon the evidence we could bring. We have his confession, of course, but a capable defending counsel could dispose of that easily enough. His wife, the only person who could testify to his identity with Samuels' nephew, could not be put into the box against him. At all events, I am disinclined to risk the experiment, especially as it would mean a most unpleasant ordeal for all concerned. What do you say, Harold?'

'I am content, if you are, sir,' said Harold absently, his eyes fixed upon April.

'And you, my dear?'

'Oh, Daddy, let them go,' replied his daughter. 'It would be too horrible. I never want to see or hear of them again.'

The Professor nodded, then looked at his watch once more. 'Dear me, it is very late!' he exclaimed. 'I told Mary not to announce dinner until I rang. You will stay with us, of course, Harold. Come, let us leave this room.'

Dinner was eaten in silence, and it was not until April had left the two men to their port that Harold found the courage to ask the question which had puzzled him since the dramatic unmasking of Denbigh.

'But how did you know that Isidore Samuels was Denbigh, sir?' he enquired, as soon as they were alone.

The Professor smiled. 'I did not *know* until he confessed it himself,' he replied. 'I deduced the probability of it in this way. As soon as I had reached the conclusion that Isidore Samuels played a dual rôle, I began to consider what his second rôle could be. And here I was greatly struck by one significant fact. In this second rôle, he was obviously concerned not to fasten upon you so much the responsibility of Samuels' death, but to bring into prominence the facts of your life which would blacken your character in the eyes of your friends. The choice of your rooms as the depository of the body cannot have been wholly chance. Then, when the article in *The Weekly Record* appeared, it was more than ever obvious that the attack upon your character was part of the mystery.

'Now, who were your friends, and what advantage could it be to anybody to discredit you in their eyes? Your associates of the Naxos Club were already sufficiently alienated by the raiding of that institution, consequent upon your examination by the police. Further, the light thrown upon your past was of a kind that would hardly shock their sensibilities. There remained only—April and myself.'

Harold gasped. 'But surely, sir—'

'Wait,' said the Professor. 'It does not take much perspicacity to see that April, although she takes her amusement where she can find it, has only really cared for one man, however unworthy of her he may have proved himself. Now in whose interest was it to degrade that man in her eyes that she must perforce abandon all memory of him? Why was it that Isidore promised to relieve his wife of his presence on the conditions she told you? Obviously because he wanted his freedom. The attempt was being made to entangle you inextricably, and at the same time to persuade April of your utter worthlessness. And if you will forgive me saying so, the attempt nearly succeeded, mainly through your own folly.

'Now and here I candidly admit my own error. I had at one time thought that Denbigh might make a suitable husband for my girl. He had completely imposed upon me, and I believed that he might persuade her to marry him. You had apparently chosen a different course to the one I had anticipated for you, and I believed that since she must marry somebody that Denbigh would prove a suitable substitute for you. Denbigh probably guessed this, and realised that his principal obstacle was her lingering affection for you. It was only logic, my dear boy, that pointed to Denbigh as being the man most interested in your effacement.

'The appearance of the newspaper article confirmed this suspicion, which, at first, I confess, I had been inclined to scout. One point about it struck me with great force. My own theories of the disappearance were to some extent borrowed, and my own line of argument employed. If Denbigh had written it, this was explained, for he had listened patiently to my remarks on the subject, and was the only person except April and yourself with whom I had discussed the case.

'But this, of course, might have been pure coincidence. It was not until the lady we knew as Miss Donaldson produced a definite fact, that of the strange birthmark, that any conclusive test of my suspicions became practicable. I determined to apply this test and to follow it with a confrontation. At my suggestion April asked Denbigh to tea this afternoon, and on my part I gave appointments to you and Miss Donaldson at definite hours later. Soon after Denbigh's appearance I devised a scheme whereby his left shoulder should come under April's observation. I preferred that the exposure of this clue should be left to her discretion. Had she decided to say nothing, to shield him, I should have deferred the revelation of his identity until I had had an opportunity of consulting her wishes.'

'By Jove, sir, you thought of everything!' exclaimed Harold.

The Professor smiled. 'It is, perhaps, fortunate that I did,' he replied briskly. 'Now, I imagine that you and April may have a few words to say to one another. If you will take my advice, you will tell her the truth in every detail. Off you go. You will find me in the study if you want me.'

It was not until after midnight that the Professor, who had been dozing in his chair before the fire, opened his eyes and blinked as the handle of the study door turned softly. April ran across the room, and, seating herself on the arm of the chair, put her arms around him and kissed him.

'Daddy, you're a clever old darling, and I've been a silly fool,' she whispered.

'U—m,' muttered the Professor. 'And where's that young scapegrace?'

'I'm here, sir,' came Harold's voice from the doorway.

'Oh, you are?' replied the Professor severely. 'Well, you've been a fool, too. See that you don't do it again.'

THE END

THE PLAY

THE PURPLE LINE

As well as over 170 novels and novel-length works of non-fiction, John Street wrote short stories and plays for radio and the stage. His earliest known short story is 'Gunner Morson, Signaller', published in March 1918 and written for propaganda purposes. In the story, a signaller saves a group of his countrymen from an unexpected German attack and, consistent with what would become the hallmark of John Street's detective stories, kills an enemy soldier with a most unusual weapon.

Dr Lancelot Priestley, the detective in the majority of his 'John Rhode' mysteries, appeared in only two short stories, 'The Elusive Bullet' and 'The Vanishing Diamond', as a result of which they are frequently anthologised. We have therefore selected for inclusion alongside *The Paddington Mystery* Street's rarely seen final short story 'The Purple Line', which was first published in the London *Evening Standard* on 20 January 1950.

T.M.

Inspector Purley picked up the telephone. But the torrent of words which poured into his ears was so turbid that he could make little of it. Something about a wife and a water-butt. 'I'll come along at once,' said Purley. 'Holly Bungalow, you say? On the Cadford Road? Right!'

He took the police car, in which he drove out of the fair-sized market town of Faythorpe. The villas on the outskirts extended for a short distance, with a scarlet telephone kiosk near the further end.

It was growing dark on a February afternoon, and it was pouring with rain.

About half a mile beyond the kiosk he saw, on the left, a white-painted gate between the trees and standing beside it, a man with a bicycle. The inspector saw 'Holly Bungalow' painted on the gate.

As he got out of the car, the man at the gate began gabbling and gesticulating. He was short and stocky. He wore a mackintosh, sodden with wet, and was hatless, with the rain pouring from his hair over his face.

'Rode at once to the kiosk,' he was rambling incoherently. 'That's where I rang you up from. We're not on the telephone, you know. I didn't know what else to do. It's a dreadful thing. Come, I'll show you.'

At the back of the bungalow was a verandah, looking out over a lawn and garden surrounded by trees. At the further end of the verandah was a round galvanised water-butt, overflowing with the water pouring into it from a spout in the eaves. Projecting from the top of the butt, and resting against the edge was a pair of inverted high-heeled shoes. 'It's my wife!' the little man exclaimed.

The butt was about five feet high. Beside it was a folding wooden garden chair. Purley climbed on to this, and leaned over the edge of the butt. Within it, completely submerged but for the feet, was a woman, head down and fully clothed

The first problem was how to get her out. He tilted the butt till it fell on its side.

The little man made no attempt to help Purley as he drew the woman out by the legs. She was fairly tall and slim, apparently in the thirties, wearing a dark frock, silk stockings and high-heeled shoes, with no hat.

Purley glanced into the butt. The water had drained out of it, and all it now contained was a layer of slime and a broken ridge-tile, which had at some time presumably fallen into it from the roof.

Purley carried the body into the shelter of the verandah. The little man was quivering like a jelly. 'You'd better come with me,' said Purley.

In a dazed fashion the other followed him back to the car. Purley drove to the kiosk, where he telephoned to the police station. Then the two drove back to the bungalow.

They entered by the front door. The bungalow was not large—lounge, dining-room, a couple of bedrooms. The furnishings were well-to-do. In the dining-room, a french window leading on to the verandah was open. On the table were remains of a meal, apparently lunch, with one place only laid. Beside this, a tumbler, a syphon and a bottle of whisky, half full.

As they sat down Purley took out his note-book and headed a page 'Monday, February 13'. He said: 'You told me the name was Briston, I think?'

The other nodded. 'That's right. I am Henry Briston. My wife's name was Shirley. She had seemed rather depressed for the last few days.'

'When did you last see her alive?'

'About eight o'clock this morning,' Briston replied. 'She was in bed then. I got up early, for I was going to Mawnchester to see my brother, and I took her a cup of tea. She seemed quite cheerful then. I got my own breakfast, and while the egg was frying I put a new chart in the barograph yonder.'

He pointed to the instrument on a bracket fixed to the dining-room wall. Purley was familiar with barographs—there was one in the window of the optician's next door to the police station. The one on the wall was of the conventional type, with a revolving drum driven by clockwork, and a pen at the end of a long needle. The chart stuck round the drum bore out Briston's words. It ran from Monday to Sunday, ruled in two-hour divisions, the lines an eighth of an inch apart.

The pen had been set at eight o'clock that morning, and filled rather clumsily, for the deep purple oily ink had overflowed and run vertically down the chart. The time was now seven o'clock, and the pen pointed correctly between the six and eight o'clock lines. The graph it had drawn ran horizontally for an eighth of an inch, from eight to ten. After that time it sloped steeply downwards, indicating rapidly falling pressure.

'And after breakfast?' Purley asked. 'You saw her again?'

'I didn't see her,' Briston replied. 'I called through the door and told her I was going, and she answered me. Then I jumped on my bicycle and rode to the station to catch the 8.50 to Mawnchester.'

'Was Mrs Briston expecting anyone to call here?'

'Not that I know of. I met the postman on the road as I was riding to the station. I called out to him if he had anything for me, and he said only a parcel for my wife.'

'Was that garden chair standing by the water butt when you left home?'

'I don't think so. If it was, I didn't put it there. At this time of year it's kept folded up in the verandah. I sometimes use it to stand on and look into the butt to see how much water there is. But this morning the butt was empty. During the dry spell we had last week, we used all the water for the greenhouse. It would have taken three or four hours to fill even with the heavy rain today.'

'Did you put this bottle of whisky on the table here?'

'No, I found it there when I came home. Latterly, my wife had taken to drinking rather more than I liked to see. I didn't clear away my breakfast things before I left this morning. My wife must have done that, and got her own lunch later on.'

'You went to Mawnchester by the 8.50. What time did you come back?'

'By the train that gets to Faythorpe at 4.45. The ticket collector will remember that—we had some conversation. I had taken a cheap day ticket, but it wasn't available for return as early as the 4.45, and I had to pay the full fare. I lunched with my brother in Mawnchester and saw several other people there.'

There came a loud knock. Purley opened the door, to find the divisional surgeon. 'This way, doctor,' he said. 'What can you tell me?'

'Not very much more than you can see for yourself,' said the doctor. 'She's been dead some hours. Death was due to drowning. There's a pretty severe contusion on the top of the head. It wouldn't have been fatal, for the skull isn't fractured. But you'll want to account for it, I expect.'

'Have a look inside the butt,' said Purley. 'You see that broken ridge-tile?'

The doctor nodded. 'Yes, I see it. You found her head downwards in the butt, you say? If, when she dived in, her head had struck the tile, the contusion would be accounted for.'

Purley went back to Faythorpe. Accident, murder, or suicide? The only way she could have fallen headlong into the butt by accident was if she had been clambering about on the roof; such behaviour might surely be ruled out.

Murder? By whom? Her husband's alibi seemed perfectly good, though, of course, it would have to be checked. And there was this finally convincing point. Nobody, certainly not her puny little husband, could have lifted a struggling victim above his shoulders and plunged her head downwards into the butt.

Suicide, then. Everything pointed to that. The depression from which Shirley Briston had been suffering. And possibly the whisky to supply Dutch courage. It had started to rain about half past nine that morning, and had never ceased all day. Three or four hours, Briston had said. The butt would have been full by the time she might be expected to have had her lunch. She had taken out the garden chair, climbed on to it, and dived into the butt.

Verification of Briston's alibi followed naturally. The ticket collector remembered him perfectly well. 'I couldn't say what train he went by in the morning, for I wasn't on duty then,' he told Purley. 'But he came off the 4.45 and gave up the return half of a cheap date to Mawnchester. I told him that was no good, as cheap tickets are only available by trains leaving Mawnchester after six. So he paid me the difference, and I gave him a receipt for it.'

Purley ran the postman to earth in the bar of the Red Admiral. 'This morning's delivery?' he replied to Purley's question. 'Yes, I do recollect seeing Mr Briston while I was on my way to Cadford. He was riding his bike towards the town here, and as he passed he called out and asked me if I had anything for him. I told him that all there was for Holly Bungalow was a parcel for Mrs Briston.'

'You delivered the parcel, I suppose?' Purley remarked. 'Did you see anyone at the bungalow?'

'Why, yes,' the postman replied. 'I knocked on the door. Mrs Briston opened it. She wasn't properly dressed, but had a sort of wrap round her.'

'Can you tell me what time this was?'

'It must have been round about half-past eight when I spoke to Mr Briston. And maybe five minutes later when I got to the bungalow.'

All that remained was a final word with the doctor. There

was just one possibility. Briston had arrived at Faythorpe station at 4.45. He should have reached home by 5.15. It had been after six when Purley had first seen the body in the butt. Only the faintest possibility, of course.

The doctor was at home when Purley called and frowned irritably at his question. 'How the dickens can I tell to a split second? I'm ready to testify on oath that death was due to drowning. But I'm not prepared to say exactly when it took place. When a body has been in water for any length of time, that's impossible. My opinion is that the woman died not later than midday or thereabouts.'

So that settled it. Mrs Briston had been seen alive after her husband left the house. The medical evidence showed that she must have been dead before his return that evening. Clearly, then, suicide.

Next morning, Pursley went to Holly Bungalow fairly early. The door was opened by a man who bore some resemblance to Henry Briston. 'Do you want see my brother?' he asked. 'I am Edward Briston, from Mawnchester. Henry rang me up last night, and told me what had happened, and I came over at once. He's had a very bad night, and I told him he'd better stay in bed for a bit.'

'I won't disturb him,' Purley replied. 'I only looked in to see he was all right. You saw your brother in Mawnchester yesterday, didn't you?'

'Yes, he lunched with me, and we spent the afternoon together in my office, till he left to catch his train.'

Purley nodded. 'Have you any personal knowledge of your sister-in-law's state of mind?'

Edward Briston glanced over his shoulder, led the way into the dining-room and shut the door. 'It was to talk about Shirley that Henry came to see me yesterday,' he said in a hushed voice. 'He told me she was terribly depressed. As it she had something on her mind that she wouldn't tell him.

'I'm going to tell you something, inspector, that I didn't tell Henry, and never shall now. One day last week I saw Shirley in Mawnchester. She was with a man I didn't know, and they seemed to be getting on remarkably well together. I know she saw me, but the couple hurried away together in the opposite direction. It's my belief the poor woman had got herself into a situation from which she could see only one way of escape.'

That might be the case, Purley thought. Glancing round the room he caught sight of the barograph. After that flat step, an eighth of an inch wide, the purple line traced by the pen had fallen steadily till about midnight. Then it had become horizontal, and was now beginning to rise. Fine weather might be expected.

The prosperous appearance of the room prompted Purley's next question. 'Your brother is in comfortable circumstances?'

'Well, yes,' Edward Briston replied. 'Henry hasn't much of his own, but Shirley had considerable means. She was a widow when he married her, and her first husband had left her quite well off.'

Henry Briston's alibi was complete. There could be no doubt now that his wife had committed suicide, and Edward Briston's guess might explain why.

Purley went back to the police station and caught sight of the barograph in the window next door.

He looked at the instrument more closely. It was very similar to the one at Holly Bungalow, the only difference that Purley could see was the chart on the drum, which ran from Sunday to Saturday. A new chart had been fitted at 10 o'clock the previous Sunday, for that was where the purple graph began. For the greater part of Sunday it ran almost horizontally. Then, late that evening, it began to decline. By the early hours of Monday morning this decline had become a steep slope.

As with the instrument at Holly Bungalow, this fall had continued till about midnight.

The queer thing about this graph was that it showed no horizontal step between eight and ten on Monday morning. Briston's barograph must be out of order. But it couldn't be, for in every other respect the two purple lines were exactly similar.

Purley went into the police station. A discrepancy only an eighth of an inch long in the graphs could be of no importance. And then the only possible explanation revealed itself.

His thoughts began to race. There was no confirmation of Henry Briston having left Faythorpe by the 8.50. He had certainly been seen by the postman riding in the direction of the station about 8.30. But he might have turned back when the postman had passed the bungalow on his way back to Cadford. A later train would have given him plenty of time to meet his brother for lunch.

Back to the bungalow, to find his wife dressed and having breakfast. Perhaps he had contrived to meet the postman. He could easily have ordered something to be sent her by post. That contusion the doctor had found. The kitchen poker! A blow, not enough to kill her, but to knock her out.

But it would manifestly have been beyond Briston's power to lift even an inert body over the edge of the butt. No, it wouldn't do. By jove, yes, it would! It hadn't begun to rain till 9.30, and before then the butt had been empty. Briston had tipped the butt over on its side.

First the broken tile, to explain the contusion that must be found. Then the unconscious woman, dragged through the french window of the dining-room and thrust head first into the butt.

An effort, and the butt with its contents was upended in place. Perhaps the rain water was already beginning to trickle into it from the spout.

Then to set the scene, so as to suggest that the victim had been alive at a much later hour. To clear away the breakfast, and to lay the appearance of lunch, with the significant whisky bottle.

In his preoccupation with the crime, he had forgotten to change the barograph chart. It was by then ten o'clock. He put on a new chart, and set the pen on the eight o'clock line, to suggest the time of his action. Then he turned the drum till the pen rested on the ten o'clock line.

He was bound to do that, otherwise it might be noticed later that the instrument was two hours slow. That was the only possible explanation of the purple line being horizontal for a vital eighth of an inch.

The motive might be deduced from Edward Briston's revelation. The only evidence for Shirley Briston's depressed state was her husband's. She hadn't been depressed, but determined. She had told him she was going to leave him. And if she did that, her money would go with her.

It was beyond any doubt that the barograph had been set, not at eight, but at ten. If it could be proved that Henry Briston had set it, his alibi was destroyed. He must have been in a state of great agitation. He had clumsily overfilled the pen, so that the ink had run down the chart. Might he not in his agitation have got some of it on his fingers? That oily purple fluid was not a true ink, but a dye, defying soap and water.

Purley drove again to Holly Bungalow. This time Henry Briston himself opened the door. 'Hold out your hands, Mr Briston,' said the inspector.

'My hands?' Briston replied. He held them out tremblingly, palms downwards. Purley seized the right hand and turned it over. There on the inner side of forefinger and thumb were two faint purple stains.

'Come with me,' said Purley sternly. 'And I must caution you—'

THE END

MYSTERY AT OLYMPIA

*'Readers know well what to expect from John Rhode, and in this
story they will not be disappointed . . . The tale is neat and clear
and logical, and there are no loose ends.'*
TIMES LITERARY SUPPLEMENT

The new Comet was fully expected to be the sensation of the
annual Motor Show at Olympia. Suddenly, in the middle of the
dense crowd of eager spectators, an elderly man lurched forward
and collapsed in a dead faint. But Nahum Pershore had not
fainted. He was dead, and it was his death that was to provide
the real sensation of the show.

A post-mortem revealed no visible wound, no serious organic
disorder, no evidence of poison. Doctors and detectives were
equally baffled, and the more they investigated, the more insol-
uble the puzzle became. Even Dr Lancelot Priestley's un-rivalled
powers of deduction were struggling to solve this case.

*'Mystery at Olympia is, of course, admirably pieced together.
One expects that of Mr Rhode; but it also marks an advance in
the psychological treatment of his characters.'*
ILLUSTRATED LONDON NEWS

INVISIBLE WEAPONS

'John Rhode never lets you down. A carefully worked out plot, precise detection, with no logical flaws or jumping to conclusions, and enough of character and atmosphere to carry the thing along.'
FRANCIS ILES in the *DAILY TELEGRAPH*

The murder of old Mr Fransham while washing his hands in his niece's cloakroom was one of the most astounding problems that ever confronted Scotland Yard. Not only was there a policeman in the house at the time, but there was an ugly wound in the victim's forehead and nothing in the locked room that could have inflicted it.

The combined efforts of Superintendent Hanslet and Inspector Waghorn brought no answer and the case was dropped. It was only after another equally baffling murder had been committed that Dr Lancelot Priestley's orderly and imaginative deductions began to make the connections that would solve this extraordinary case.

'Any murder planned by Mr Rhode is bound to be ingenious.'
OBSERVER

THE ROGUES' SYNDICATE

FRANK FROËST and
GEORGE DILNOT

Lost in a London fog, young Jimmie Hallett is accosted by a frightened woman who hands him a package and flees. Within hours, he is being questioned about the murder of the girl's father and a dangerous international conspiracy. Can genial detective Weir Menzies, even with all the resources of Scotland Yard behind him, succeed in outwitting a faceless gang of organised thieves and killers?

Frank Froëst, the highly decorated Superintendent of Scotland Yard's C.I.D., began his retirement from the Metropolitan Police by writing *The Grell Mystery*, acclaimed as the first crime novel to incorporate authentic police procedures. With George Dilnot, co-author of the story collection *The Crime Club*, Froëst wrote one more novel, the ambitious and thrilling *The Rogues' Syndicate*.

'A police "procedural" from 1916. Loved the jargon—kind of a tough 1930's gangster, British style. Loved the story . . . Another fun read from a completely different time.'
GOODREADS

MR BOWLING BUYS A NEWSPAPER

DONALD HENDERSON

'*I have a book called* Mr Bowling Buys a Newspaper *which I have read half a dozen times and have bought right and left to give away. I think it is one of the most fascinating books written in the last ten years and I don't know anybody in my limited circle who doesn't agree with me.*'
RAYMOND CHANDLER

Mr Bowling is getting away with murder. On each occasion he buys a newspaper to see whether anyone suspects him. But there is a war on, and the clues he leaves are going unnoticed. Which is a shame, because Mr Bowling is not a conventional serial killer: he *wants* to get caught so that his torment can end. How many more newspapers must he buy before the police finally catch up with him?

'*Henderson pursues a grim little theme with lively perception and ingenuity. His manner is brief, deliberately undertoned, and for the most part curiously effective.*'
TIMES LITERARY SUPPLEMENT